LITTLE GEORGE AND THE GRAND-NITE- CHAMPION

By

VERLAN LAFLEUR

CHAPTER 1

Flat Creek

Bouncing his old basketball three times on the hard packed dirt of the barn yard and taking carful aim at the rim, Little George bends his knees. As he straightens his legs back up he releases the ball.

As the ball sails through the air and makes a perfect arch, it comes down and hits the front of the rim and slowly rolls "Around the World"' and falls off the edge.

"Darn it… missed again," he mutters. Then in an instance he *can* hear his mother calling him at the top of her lungs from the back door of their home.

"Little George get in this house this very minute and get yourself cleaned up. I have a 9:00 doctor appointment this morning."

Standing only five foot-four inches tall and weighing one hundred-twenty pounds with two big rocks in her back pockets. Little George's mother is known in the family as the one with a short fuse for a temper. His daddy always said he can tell when Little George's mother is mad. "Her hair turns a deeper red and the freckles sprinkled across her beautiful face lights up her face.

Usually Little George is on his daily schedule of practicing his free throws after doing his morning chores.

During a trip to town last summer his daddy bought him an old rusted basketball goal at a flea market in Oberlin. After a little prodding his daddy nailed it up on the side of the corn crib so he could practice his free throws and hook shots.

But hearing his mother calling him in her, "You're in trouble little boy," tone of voice makes Little George drop his basketball and take off running like an Olympic Sprinter.

Right now he's cutting around the tool shed with half its wooden shingles still missing from last year's hurricane.

And now he is hurdling over two and sometimes three fresh cow patties, which are in his path. Each time he jumps Little George sees little puffs of brown dust flying up around his feet.

Now he slide's to a complete stop just long enough to flip the wire latch off the white picket fence gate. Once through the gate he's running up the back steps two at a time. Before you can say "Hoop-Sha" he's out of his dust covered Brogans.

Before you know it Little George is running through the bathroom doorway. As he passes the towel rack he grabs a white wash cloth and runs water over it from the faucet.

First he starts washing behind both ears then under his neck and both arms. When he's finishes washing he notices something strange has happened to the wash cloth.

To his surprise it's changed to a dingy brown coloring. Shrugging his shoulders he figures it must be something in the water that did this to the wash cloth, because he knows for a fact he wasn't that dirty.

Shucking his faded blue jeans off and skinning out of his stretched out green and yellow John Deer Tractor Tee-Shirt, Little George wades them up into a ball and throw's them into the dirty clothes hamper.

Now he's headed for his bedroom where he snatches his new black and gold Fairview Panthers warm-ups off a cloths hanger. Next he's putting on his favorite white game tennis shoes.

On the way out of the bedroom Little George spies his silver colored Big Ben alarm clock by his bed. "All right I'm done in three minutes flat." Little George said while throwing both arms over his head and running for the door that leads to the outside.

Little George's father is just opposite of his mother. Standing six foot four inches tall with sky blue eyes and dark coal black wavy hair and a big smile a country mile wide.

He possesses the patience's of a saint, but some folks around "The Flat Creek Community'" will tell you if you rub him the wrong way. You just might have a big problem on your hands.

Joy is Little George's twin sister and best friend and confident when he needs one. The only problem with her is her ability to nag him for no earthly reason, or elbowing him upside the head while they're playing a game of one on one basketball, yet of course she is always right no matter what the case may be.

Going to town once a week is a real treat for the two of them, but going twice in one week is a special treat. While their mother is waiting to see the doctor Joy and Little George will get to walk to the "Five and Dime Store'" located on Main Street.

Once there they'll stock up on their favorite candy using the money they've earned working after school at the veterinarian clinic their daddy and grandpa own.

Running around the corner of the house Little George grabs the rear door handle of their car. Throwing it wide open he jumps in and plops down onto the rear seat next to Joy.

Joy is dressed in her new emerald green dress with white trimming around the nick. As he glances over at her he notices she is pinching her nose and giving him that stinker, nasty, critical eye of hers.

Before Little George can say a word Joy says in a criticizing voice, "Why didn't you at less run a comb through that patch of mop hair that's sitting on top your head and clean up Little George, you smell like a Boar Hog."

Giving her his best sneer face Little George growls, "I have a better idea little miss prissy. Why don't you mind your own business and shut up."

Think god their mother and daddy are walking towards the car. Because parts of Little George's life starts flashing before his eyes. Joy had already balled up her fist to hit him.

After opening the door for Little George's mother, his father walks around the car and climbs into the driver's seat. After adjusting the seat Little George's father gazes at the two of them through the rear view mirror and says, "Ok—you guys ready to head to town?"

"Yes sir," They both chime in.

CHAPTER 2

To get to Highway Twenty Six you have to endure a four mile ride on a pea gravel road loaded with pot holes and ruts. If you're lucky someone working for the parish will come and grade the road with a big yellow grader called a Galleon.

After the road is graded it will stay smooth for a week, or two, or till the next rain. Little George's neighbor, Mr. Smith once said a politician had mentioned something about black topping "The Flat Creek Road.'" Little George's daddy chuckled and said, "Don't hold your breath on that promise."

It's not unusual to have a little ground fog in late November in southwest Louisiana where there's water lying around. The weatherman on channel seven once said a ground fog can occur when the night air is cooler than the water that's in the creeks, or around where water is staying on the ground. He called it Infrared Cooling, but the folks living on Flat Creek call it, "Slow Down and Live.'" Because the cattle that are loose in the woods are mostly Brahmas and they like to lie down on the road, because the road bed is still warm from the day time sun.

The only problem with this is, the color of a Brahma is a haze gray color which mimics the color of the ground fog. But once the sun gets up above the tree tops the ground fog will burn off and a beautiful sunny fall day will begin.

CHAPTER 3

L ittle George stretches his neck to look over the front seat so he can get a better view of where they are on the road. And he spies his favorite part of the ride coming up "The Flat Creek Bridge.'"

To make crossing the bridge more interesting one has to know at what speed he has to travel so that when the front of the car rolls up onto the end of the bridge, it will cause the car to bolt up into the air, thus giving a person a few seconds of feeling weightless. Little George can see a big grin on his daddy's face in the rearview mirror. Their daddy knows Joy and Little George looks forward to their "Hang Time'" as he calls it.

"Ok...Here comes the bridge. Now hold on tight," Little George's father says.

The car makes a loud thud as the front of the car rolls up onto the end of the bridge.

As the car shots up into the air Little George gazes over at Joy as she giggles for all it's worth. And they both let out a loud, "Waa-Woo!!"

As the car comes back down to earth and the dust settles Little George hears a blood curdling scream coming from the front of the car which sounds like his mother's voice.

Now the sounds of blaring horns along with the screeching noise of tires on the graveled road fill the air.

Out of the corner of his eye he spies a large, red logging truck materializing out of the hazy gray ground fog.

Little George reaches over to grab Joy, but before he can reach her she disappears from his sight. Only the look of horror, that was painted across her face remains with him.

Then a large dark brown object hits him in the chest with such force it throws his body hard against the back seat.

Trying to look around, all he can see are small particles of glass flying through the air resembling crystal bullets.

As he looks up Little George glimpse the sun somersaulting through the clear blue sky. But his mind is racing, trying to grasp what in the world is happing and, when will it stop? Where did Joy go? And why did his mother scream so loud? How on earth did the big logging truck get in the road? Yet no one is saying a word.

As the car whirls and tumbles through the air he feels a white hot burning sensation traveling down his right leg.

Even with all of this happing Little George knows his mouth is wide open and he is trying with all his strength to scream out, but nothing comes out. Before his last breath of air is sucked from his lungs Little George can see a kaleidoscope of red and yellow lights swirling around him. Then total darkness and peaceful quite envelope's him.

CHAPTER 4

The Hospital

In Little George's subconscious mind he can hear a soft and gentle voice saying, "You can do it son." The voice keeps echoing from far away. Now he feels a tapping sensation on the back of his right hand.

Slowly at first then a little at a time a thick dark veil begins to lift. Now he feels his eyes trying to make a connection as they flutter open.

He can now see his Grandmother Gracie dabbing a white lace handkerchief at a tear welling up in her beautiful hazel eyes. As always her snow white hair is perfectly combed and a slight hint of perfume floats on the air.

As Little George move's his head on the pillow a shock of pain shoots through his body and he almost lose conscious. After a short while Little George catches his breath and tries adjusting his eyes. He can see a large bright florescent light fixture hanging from a snow white ceiling.

In a short minute his nose picks up the strange scent of

medicine and disinfects. To his surprise his voice kicks in. And with a drowsy voice he says, "Where am I? What happened?"

Grandma Gracie sucks in a deep breath and mutters, "There was a horrible accident on The Flat Creek Bridge."

Little George gazes up into his Grandma Gracie's eyes and in a choking voice, "Where is daddy, mother and Joy?"

"What you need right now Little George is lots of rest and the answers to your questions will gradually come to you," A deep voice said.

Shifting his head as far as the pain will let him in the direction of the voice.

There standing by the window Little George spies his Grandpa Big George

Some of the folks living on Flat Creek say, "The only way to tell Little George's father from his father is. Big George wear's Ben Franklin eye glasses and Little George's father doesn't wear glasses."

Shifting his gaze up to the ceiling and staring at the light for a short second Little George mumbles softly, "What if I told you what happened... after all I was there."

Seeing the shock registering on his grandparents faces as he makes this statement, Little George knows he has to know what happened to his parents and sister.

After a few minutes of prodding Grandma Gracie brakes down in tears. And in between her sobbing she fills Little George in on the missing pieces.

Grandpa George tries with all of his might to remain strong throughout Grandma Gracie's telling Little George of the deaths of his love one's. But in the end he couldn't stand up through the pain and sorrow of losing his only son, daughter-in-law, and grandchild he loves so much. "What god has taken away from us, he has all so given back to us," Grandpa George stammers as he walks out of the room with his big shoulders bent.

CHAPTER 5

From his hospital bed room window Little George can see a bright crimson sunset in the making. His Grandpa George once told him when he was in the navy and you saw a red sunset there was a saying that went like this, "Red sky at night sailor's delight. Red sky in the morning sailor's take warning." Little George often wondered about this saying and just what it's meaning?

After a nurse comes in and gives him a pain pill, it seems like in a matter of minutes Little George's eye lids began to feel like they weight a ton.

As the room gets darker, he can hear a rustling noise outside his window. Glancing in the direction of the noise, he spies a "Red Breasted Robin'" perched on the window ledge looking in at him. And every now and then it will peck at the window then turn its head sideways and blink its coal black eyes in his direction.

CHAPTER 6

The next morning Nurse Anna comes in to take Little George's temperature and pulse.

Dressed in a bright white Nurse's uniform and her long blond hair tied up in a bun. Nurse Anna has a feeling, that the little red headed boy she is looking at needs a little cheering up. During their conversation Little George happens to mention about his late evening visitor. Looking up from the clip board she's writing on. Little George spies a smile forming on Nurse Anna's face as she says, "Well it looks like you have a guardian angel watching over you Little George."

"A guardian angel?"

"Yep...that's what I said. You're one of the lucky few, because he's a very special bird. The staff here at the hospital named him Monk."

"Monk. What a weird name for a bird."

"Maybe so, but you see no one's ever heard him sing. And he always hangs out around the hospital even, when all the other birds have migrated south for the winter. But Old Monk stays right here."

"I wonder why?"

"Some of us believe he stays to watch over those patients, who are critical, or, who needs a little extra watching over."

After hooking the brown clip board back at the foot of Little George's hospital bed. Nurse Anna heads through the doorway. And as she looks over her shoulder she says, "And that's how he got his name."

CHAPTER 7

As the lights in the hospital hallways are dimed for the night, things quiet down. It's then Little George decides to give himself a physical checkup. Starting at the top of his head he finds a bump about the size of a golf ball, which still aches a little, when he touches it.

Next up he feels a few Band-Aids covering some scratches on his Cheeks and Chin.

After flexing his arms and moving his shoulders. Little George decides not to prolong this part of his checkup. After all he can move them even though both arms are loaded with Catheters.

After catching his breath he moves his hand over his chest area. There he feels a knot with bandages covering his entire chest area.

Knowing he can't reach his legs. Little George figures he can at least move one then the other.

So he tell his brain to move his left leg please. And it does move on its own, but the pain almost causes him to pass out.

Taking a deep breath Little George reaches over for a Kleenex on the stand next to his bed and dabs at the sweat that's popped out on his forehead from that move.

After taking a couple of deep breaths he grabs the side rails of his hospital bed. Now he tells his brain to please move his right leg. After a few seconds it dawns on Little George nothing moved. He looks at the white blanket covering his body and in horror he yells out at the top of his lungs, "What in the world happened to my right leg. Where is it!!?"

The next thing Little George spies, when he opens his eyes is his hospital room is full of people wearing white coats and white dresses.

In a short few second he feels a stinging sensation in his right arm. Then in a few seconds a numbing feeling is rushing throughout his body.

Somewhere in the distance he can hear a voice saying, "You're doing alright Little George. Now hold still please."

CHAPTER 8

The next morning Little George feels a warming sensation on his face. Slowly he cracks one eye lid half open and gazes at his window.

Someone has pulled the curtain wide open to let the sun shine into the room making Little George's room seem very warm and bright.

After a moment his ears pick up the noises of three soft pecks on one of the window panes. As he shifts his gaze a little. Little George spies Monk looking at him through his coal black eyes, which have a ring of gold coloring around them. After a few minutes of Monk and Little George staring at each other Monk spreads his wings and swirls off the window ledge. Thinking to himself Little George mumbles, "I guess he has other patients to check up on?"

At 7:00 sharp breakfast is severed whether you want it or not. In Little Georges case he definitely can live without it. Staring at a tray of powered eggs, and a glass of powdered milk, with a half slice of burnt toast. It just doesn't take long to lose your appetite.

Mary his favorite "Candy Striper'" comes into his room to take his tray away and says, "From the looks of this tray you shouldn't have to worry about being obese Little George."

Giving her his best deer in the head lights look Little George replies, "You know how boys are. We don't want to lose our teenage figure."

As she walks out the door with the tray in her hands, he hears her muttering, "My...my, but you're in a grumpy mood today."

Little George rolls over onto his left side as much as the pain will allow him. Once he gets comfortable. He starts playing a mind game with himself. Now that he's made Mary mad and Mrs. Anna his nurse thinks he's a prime basket case who needs a bird for a guardian angel. And...oh yea how about that slop they give you and call it food. Or that god forsaken I.V.PUMP that squeaks, groans, and beeps all night long while he's trying to sleep in between the nurses coming in and checking his blood pressure and temperature.

Not paying attention to his surrounding, he's brought back to reality by a feminine voice saying, "And how are you doing this bright and beautiful morning Little George?"

Hearing this jolts him back to reality. Looking at the person standing at the foot of the bed dressed in a white starched and ironed nurse's uniform, with a brass name tag, which has the name Appleton written in bold, black, block, lettering. And her long blond hair tied up in a bun with a funny little white cap perched on top her head. And her piercing blue eyes are on him.

Giving her the once over as she stands there with his clip board in one hand and the other on her hip Little George replies, "Oh not too bad for the shape I'm in." After that remark settles in George spies one of her eyebrows twitching then a small frown slowly spreads across her face.

"Ok--- from what I've gathered you've had a pretty rough night last night."

18

On the spur of the moment Little George decides to give her his old "Opossum in the Hen House Grin,'" then he says, "Maybe…just maybe it wouldn't have been quite so bad if someone would have taken a little time to set down with me and tell me I lost half of my right leg in the accident."

"I can sympathize with you Little George. Doctor Mike thought it was better to let you gain your strength back first. Then break the news of the loss of your leg. But now according to your new schedule you now have a new primary care doctor. From now on Doctor Andrew will handle your case and he should come around to see you this evening."

Nurse Appleton hangs the clip board back on the foot of his bed and turns and walks out the doorway with her starched and ironed white uniform makes a swishing noise.

With the rest of a long day ahead of him Little George would doze off and on in between blood pressure readings and temperature checks. Even the grand changing of the I.V. bottles every hour doesn't bother him anymore. He even spent a little time going over the scenes of the accident he can remember.

He remembers the car traveling down the road with a plum of dust swirling up behind it.

He can also feel the cool early morning air blowing in through the open car windows. Even the smell of dead tree leaves on the forest floor mixing in with the smell of gravel and dirt swirling up into the air as they traveled down the road.

He can even feel the sensation as the car jumps up into the air as it bounds up on to the end of the bridge. And the ear piercing screams and sounds of crushing metal are all too clear.

Even the picture of horror painted across Joy's face is imprinted in his mind. And the pain in his chest from one of the logs as it comes tearing through the car windshield. And the burning pain in his leg.

And in an instant nothing but total darkness and all of this is so surreal. Before it's all over tears are welling up in his eyes. And his throat is dry and hurting. After a short few minutes he reaches over and pours a glass of cold water from the tan plastic water pitcher, which is sitting on the small night stand by his bed.

CHAPTER 9

The word from the hospital staff is. You will hear Doctor Andrew coming before you see him. And about now Little George can hear someone humming a tune as he walks through the doorway.

When you first lay eyes on Doctor Andrews you might think you're looking at Santa Clause without the long white hair and beard. But in his effort to project a picture of medical knowledge, he's dressed in a white starched and ironed white coat with his name embroidered in blue above the top pocket of his coat. Which just happens to be filled with writing pens and thermometers. Also draped over his shoulders is a shiny new stethoscope. And he all so has on the standard white shirt, black tie alone, with the black slacks, and black loafer shoes on his feet to round out his image.

Standing at the foot of Little George's bed Doctor Andrew has his head bent down looking at Little George's chart. And every once in a while he flips a page and hums to himself. Finally after a short few minutes Doctor Andrew looks up at Little George and adjusts his Granny Glasses.

"Now let me see here. It says here you're recovering just find. But now the thought is to get you back on your feet as quickly as possible. And out of the hospital and on to a normal life."

"That's a great idea. But how my I ask are you planning

on doing this feat, when all I have is one leg?"

With that statement said Doctor Andrew's forehead suddenly furrowed in puzzlement as he stares at Little George. "Why... I guess we can start you off on a new prostatic leg for now and coupled with a little exercise to help you build up some muscle mass. Which will help you get the feeling of balance while standing up straight and walking."

"Great... I'll try anything that will help me get out of here. When can I get started?"

"Well... with that being the case. I believe we can get you started tomorrow morning bright and early," Doctor Andrew says as he replaces the clip board and spins around and heads out the doorway humming to himself again.

CHAPTER 10

Bright and early the next morning Little George is awakened by a voice that sounds like the person speaking has a mouth full of marbles.

"How are you doing this bright and beautiful morning Little George? Are you ready to start your therapy?"

Hearing this type of voice at 7:00 a.m. in a hospital puts a patient on high alert. Little George rolls over onto his side to get a better view of this person, who has invaded his peaceful sleep.

The first thing he spies is a head the size of a basketball. With brown hair on top of it and it has a Flat Top haircut. The next thing he spies is a pair of big brown eyes staring at him from under a patch of bushy brown eyebrows. From the white tee-shirt to the white pants Little George can tell this is a Jock and a Sun Worshiper in the first degree.

CHAPTER 11

Mike Strong completed a four year hitch in the Marine Corp. After getting out he applied for his Veterans Benefits. With luck on his side he was accepted into a prestigious medical school in Nashville, Tennessee and decided to take Physical Therapy.

After completing his schooling, Mike got in touch with a Marine buddy who happened to be working as a Physical Therapist at a small hospital in Southwest Louisiana.

CHAPTER 12

Letting out a big yawn and rubbing the sleep from his eyes Little George mumbles, "I didn't know therapy started this early in the day?"

After giving Little George a menacing grin. The young man introduces himself as Mike Strong. And he will be Little George's personal therapist. "You ready to tackle this job Little George?" Mike growls.

Setting up on the edge of the bed Little George gives Mike a slightly annoying look and said, "Maybe--- if they remove these I.V.'s."

◆ ◆ ◆

On the elevator ride down to the basement not a word is spoken between Mike and Little George. If tension was gun powder the whole hospital would have been leveled by now.

In his heart Little George knows Mike and he will not see eye to eye. After a slight jerk the elevator doors open up on the hospital basement floor.

Everything the human eye can see is painted a glossy white color. And lying on the floor scattered about are big black shiny rubber mats, which make the floor resemble a giant checker board.

In the middle of the room sets an array of assorted chrome bars and black pulleys hanging from the ceiling. Turning his head slowly around Little George notices not a window is to be seen. This set him to thinking maybe they don't want the outside people looking in and seeing the torture taking place down here.

Gazing around Little George can see some of the people are dressed in white like Mike. And some are dressed in green and walking around while others are setting and talking in small groups. But the big thing Little George notices first off is the smell. The odor reminds him of the dressing room of the old Fairview High School Gym. It's a sour mildew odor that hangs in the air.

As Little George's wheel chair comes to a complete stop Mike says, "Welcome to my world. I guess the first thing on the agenda is to get you fitted with a new leg. Then we can get you started off by walking and holding on to the bars."

"That would help and the sooner the better," Little George replies.

If looks could kill Little George would be one dead red headed sixteen year old kid. He knows from the start he'll never finish learning to walk on an artificial leg.

With the struggles of learning to walk again, coupled with, his mind stuck back in time. It's more than he can handle for now. Somehow he has to figure out a way to handle one problem at a time his way.

Finding a used artificial leg and showing Little George how to slip it on. Mike wheels him to the double rails. Once he's standing up Little George tries to steady himself and get the feel of standing up straight again. All the while Mike stands at the other end saying, "Ok Little George turn lose the rail and pull your right leg up and move it forward."

For some reason this command does not register in Little George's mind. With his body being weak and his head feeling dizzy he mumbles, "This ought to be more fun than a barrel full of gorillas."

After an hour of falling on his face and his butt and sweat popping out on his forehead, Little George gazes up at Mike. And in a monotone voice he says, "This is about all the fun I can stand for one day."

Once Mike has the artificial leg off, Little George wheels his wheel chair up to the elevator doors, and punches the number three on the stainless steel pad by the door. "Wait up a minute and I'll push you back to your room," Mike yells out.

Waving his arm over his head Little George shouts back, "Its ok, I can do this all by myself."

CHAPTER 13

Walking over and clapping Mike on the shoulder Larry Mott says, "Well old buddy you seem to get all the basket cases. But this time I think you got a dozy."

"I guess so. This kid has a hard row to hoe before he gets over this big hill he's built for himself. Mentally he's a total wreck and physically he's not much better off. But the one thing he has going for his self is his youth. And I hope he can use it to his advantage."

Gazing at Mike with one eye Larry ask, "In your mind you think you can pull this kid through Mike? Even with all the baggage he has."

Looking down at the floor and rubbing the back of his neck Mike replies, "Dam if I know. But I've got to give it a shot, or... what else does he have left?"

"Ok... let's roll up these mats and clock-out and I'll buy us a "Frosty-Pop-With-The-Foam-On-Top" at the old Corner Bar," Larry says.

Shrugging his shoulders Mike answers, "Sounds like a winner to me. Let's do it my boy."

CHAPTER 14

A pink glow is showing in the west. And the street lights are blinking on as Mike and Larry walk off the sidewalk and through the doorway of the Corner Bar.

Like most of the old "Honky Tonks'" the Corner Bar has seen its better days. Gone are the Army G.I.'s. and Sailors of World War Two, and the Korean War Solder's, who came in and filled the jukebox, and pool table to the brim with twenty five cent coins.

They would drink ice cold beer in the summer to stay cool. And drink eighty six proof whiskey in the winter to help fight the chill running through their bones.

The only things left now is the odors of cigarette smoke, and stale beer, which hangs in the air. And if you look around you'll see hanging on the dark wooden walls the political posters of long forgotten politicians.

An old Wurlitzer Jukebox is setting in the far corner of a small wooden dance floor with its red, gold, and white neon lights blinking off and on and belting out a song about a true love gone bad.

Larry cast an eye at Mike and mumbles, "Well it sounds like somebody's crying in their beer tonight."

"That's all I need after an hour with Little George," Mike mutters.

Glancing at Mike over the top of his beer Larry says, "Sometimes I think you take your cases to serious Mike. If a patient wants to do it they will at least try."

Mike takes a deep pull on his frosted glass mug full of drift beer. And setting it down on the wooden bar top watching the frost melt and leave wet dimples on the bar. "You just might be right."

Smiling back at Mike and shaking his head. "But knowing you like I do you'll keep on trying till you burn out."

With a tired grin on his face Mike looks up at the black lights above the bar. "You know me pretty darn good don't you?"

"Let's just say a little. I'll get the next round. Then I'm headed home and to bed."

"I'm right behind you. Tomorrow will be another fun filled day with Little George the Horrible."

"If there's a hell on earth, it's down in that basement workout room," Larry remarks.

CHAPTER 15

After two weeks of first trying to encourage Little George and almost having an all-out fist fight coupled with a few cuss outs Mike finally gives up.

Gazing at Mike seated on his office couch. Doctor Andrew adjust his Granny eye glasses. He has a feeling that Mike Strong is at his wits end. "Don't beat yourself up Mike. It's not you. Little George has a long way to go. But right now he thinks we're trying to push him and he resents our efforts. I believe the best thing to do is discharge him and let him find his own way."

Rubbing the back of his neck Mike replies, "I agree with you Doctor Andrew. It's just that I hate to lose a patient especially one, who needs so much help."

"I know how you feel Mike. Once I had a patient that had more of a mental problem than a physical problem."

Mike looks up at Doctor Andrew. "How did you deal with that person's problem?"

"There's really no way to deal with a person's internal problems. Because most of the time they hold you and me at arm's length. But given a little time with someone in their family and allowing them to talk to their family members they somehow work it out."

"And you plan is to discharge Little George to a member of his family?"

"I think so Mike. He has his grandmother and grandfather, who can work with him. And in the long run if luck works its way in. He just might try the leg on again."

Mike shakes his head up and down. "I hope so Doctor Andrew." With that said Mike gets up and walks out the door.

CHAPTER 16

In just over two weeks Little George has managed to alienate everyone around him. Starting with the doctors, nurses, therapist, and candy stripers, even Monk who doesn't check in on him anymore, all because of the excuse he uses in trying to walk on a prostatic leg.

It's like trying to walk on the frozen deck of a ship that's rolling in high seas. No matter which way you lean it's the wrong way. And you can forget about bending down to pick something up off the floor, or if you have in mind to run, or jump you can forget that too. So what is the use in trying to walk on an artificial leg?

Right now Little George is working on getting out of the hospital. Even though, he'll have to live with his grandparents on Flat Creek. In his mind he knows he'll be confined to a wheel chair for the rest of his life.

No more deer hunting with his friends, or walks in the woods. Let along playing sports like Basketball, or Volleyball. And you can forget Field and Track, or just running around. With a little luck his Grandpa George may let him help out at his Veterinary clinic. As for going back to school, it will be far into the future.

CHAPTER 17

"**I**s this Mr. George Senor?" The voice on the other end of the telephone line inquires.

"You got him. How may I help you?"

"This is Doctor Andrew... I'm Little George's primary care doctor. And I've been going over his latest progress report. And I thought, I should call and bring you up to speed on where he's at on his rehabilitation."

"Sounds like a winner to me Doctor Andrew, but let me sit down before you start."

Clearing his throat and shuffling some paper work around on his desk. Doctor Andrew says in a tired voice, "Please excuse the noise Mr. George. Ok now I have it.

From the paper work I've gotten from his therapist and others, who are involved with Little George's rehabilitation effort. It seems as though he's gone as far as he wants to go at this point in time. And the word I get is he's frustrated with trying to walk on his new prosthetic. And now he demands us to discharge him as soon as possible."

Letting out a slow breath of air, and raising his arm over his head, Big George says, "All right doctor. I could see this coming around the bend. Now how does Gracie and I fit in?"

"Well…before I discharge him tomorrow morning. I was wondering if you and your wife could come in a little early for a set down talk in my office. Maybe we can all come up with a plan to help Little George get over the rough spots and get him pointed in the right direction."

"I don't see why not. What time would be convenient for you?"

"If it's ok with you guys how about 9:00 in the morning?"

"See you then."

As Big George lays the black telephone receiver back in its cradle he has a forlorn feeling deep inside. Could this be the beginning of a long journey for Gracie and him? Or a long walk off a short pier? Either way he knows in his heart he and Gracie will do whatever it going to take to save their only grandchild.

CHAPTER 18

At 4:00 p.m. Big George turns the lock on the big red wooden doors of his veterinarian clinic. It's been a long and busy day. And from the looks of things to come he and Gracie will be burning the midnight oil again tonight. Getting into his Nineteen-Fifty-Five Red International Pickup Truck and inserting the key into the ignition and pulling out the choke. Big George turns the key on.

After the engine turns over a few times, the big flathead six cylinder engine roars to life. Grabbing the big white steering wheel with one hand and pushing the clutch in with his left foot. Big George eases the floor shifter into first gear.

Driving west on Highway Twenty Six with the sun in his face. He reaches up and lowers the sun visor to block out the suns glair.

The last two months have really taken its toll on him and Gracie. With the loss of their only begotten son, and the loss of Jean the loving mother of their only granddaughter, who always gave him hugs, and kisses, and whispered in his ear, "I love you grandpa."

Even after the funerals of his love ones there have been long and restless nights. It's been an uphill battle trying to get back to a normal way of life. Even as Christmas came and went it was the first time in his sixty-three years of life on this earth that a Christmas tree was not up in the family home. And with other holidays, yet to come Big George feels the pain of the loss of his family even more.

Dabbing at a tear with a red handkerchief, Big George pulls the big white steering wheel of the truck hard to the right.

Bouncing over the wooden cattle guard and driving down a pea gravel driveway for two hundred yards. He parks underneath the Porte co-Chere.

Gracie is standing at the kitchen window rinsing a few dishes. She watches as her husband of forty-eight years parks his truck and slides off the seat and closes the door.

Big George turns around and gives her a wink with one of his blue eyes but his body language tells her he's carrying a heavy load of grief on his big shoulders.

From the looks of things to come tonight will be spent talking and trying to solve the many mysteries of life and death.

Walking through the kitchen doorway with his old green faded John Deer Tractor cap in his hand, Big George ask, "And may I ask you how your day has been my dear?"

Wrapping her arms around her husband's nick and giving him a big hug. "Wow...flatter around here will get you a good hot supper Mr."

CHAPTER 19

After a big helping of Chicken, Sausage Jambalaya, Big George would normally be ready for a hot bath and a little football, or basketball, which ever happens to be on the old "Zenith"' black and white T.V. Then after the game, it's hit the bed and snuggle up to Gracie under a pile of homemade quilts.

But that won't happen tonight. After the table is cleared off and the dishes are cleaned, dried, and put up in their place. Big George and Gracie walk hand and hand into the living room.

Gracie slides her hickory rocker chair closer to Big George's big mahogany colored recliner. She had started a fire in the big stone fireplace early to take the chill out of the house and now only the embers remain.

After a few minutes of talking about his day at work, Big George looks at Gracie. "Well Old Lady of mine," he said with affection in his voice. "I got a phone call from Little George's doctor this afternoon. A doctor by the name of Andrew and he wants to have a set-down talk with you and me tomorrow morning. It seems our grandson has about all he can stand of that hospital. And the good doctor thinks it may be a good idea to release him."

"I figured you might get a call about Little George," Gracie's voice stammers unevenly.

Looking at the woman he married at the age of seventeen. "Ok… can I get in on this top secret development?"

"Yes you can Old Man of mine. Last week while I was at the hospital watching one of Little George's walking sections. I was surprised, when he snapped at one of his therapist. Then I started wondering what else can be going on. Well… on my way out I ran into Lou-Ann. After we talked a bit I explained what I'd seen and I asked her to keep me informed on any problems with Little George."

Pushing his recliner back as far as it will go and placing both hands behind his head and interlocking his fingers Big George inquires, "And did Miss Lou-Ann find out anything we should know?"

"Yep… She sure did. And from what she told me over the phone. I believe what we have on our hands is not only a grandson who's handicap. But a grandson with a truck load of emotional problems too, my Old Man."

"I kind of figured the emotional problems are going to be the tuff ones for him to get over. But we have to give it a try my Old Lady. He's the only family we have left."

Gazing at her husband with a gleam in her hazel eyes Gracie reaches out and slaps Big George on the knee and said, "Ok Old Man. I'm heading for the bathroom and a good soaking. Then this chick is off to bed."

"Good Night. After the ten-o-clock news is over this old rooster is heading to bed too."

CHAPTER 20

The next morning at 5:30 sharp Sammie's up on a fence post outside Big George and Gracie's bedroom window crowing his heart out.

Big George roll's over and wipes the sleep from his eyes and yawns and mumbles, "I wonder if there's a great demand for a "Rhode Island Red Rooster'" any where's in the world."

"I doubt it. That's why we have Sammy Old Man of mine," Gracie says over her shoulder as she closes the bathroom door.

After breakfast and the animals are fed and watered. Big George and Gracie point the pickup truck east on Highway-Twenty-Six.

Coming up on the "Whisky Chitto Creek Bridge,'" Big George lets up on the gas pedal. Once the truck reach's the center of the bridge he puts the truck into neutral. Big George looks down at the creek with its gently flowing current and snowy white sand bars. The scene reminds him of happier times, when Gracie and George Junior and him spent the day picnicking, fishing, and swimming in its cool water. And the time they buried a watermelon in the sand by the water's edge for it to cool from the heat of the day.

Then Big George cut the big light green "Charleston Gray'" watermelon with his "Old Timer'" pocket knife. And they ate it right there on the sand bar.

Out of the corner of her eye Gracie notices Big George gazing at the big white sand bar. After a short minute of silence she says, "You got that faraway look in your eyes my Old Man. Can you be thinking of the day we picnicked on that big sand bar and we ate that big watermelon? And after we finished it we threw watermelon seeds at each other."

"You could always read my mind my Old Lady," Big George says as he uses a finger to wipe a tear away.

Shifting the truck into first gear Big George lets up on the clutch. As the truck picks up speed, Gracie spies a faint grin on Big George's face.

For the rest of the trip Gracie and Big George doesn't say a word. They spend their time gazing out the truck windows at the pine trees speeding by and loss in their own thoughts.

CHAPTER 21

"Please have a seat folks. I thought since you're Little George's maternal grandparents. And his primary care givers it would be in your best interest and his. That we meet and I share some of my observations and findings on his recovery effort with you folks," Doctor Andrew said with a concerned voice.

Hunching his big shoulders and staring at a picture hanging on the wall behind Doctor Andrew desk showing a navy destroyer in a battle scene. Big George says, "Doctor Andrew you're a doctor of human medicine and I'm a doctor of veterinarian medicine. Now the only thing that separates the two is. You deal with humans and me with animals. But the one fact that runs common with humans and animals is the fact both have the ability to grieve."

Doctor Andrews glances over the top of his granny eye glasses at Big George. "I whole heartily agree with you Mr. George.

As for me I can't even imagine the pain you and Gracie must feel right now. Not only did you two lose a loving son, but you all so lost a daughter-in-law, and a precious granddaughter. And now you are both faced with the greatest task of all. How do you keep from losing Little George your only grandchild?"

Looking through tears welling up in her eyes Gracie says in a choking voice, "I don't know about you two doctors, but I couldn't stand to lose my only grandchild."

Reaching over his desk Doctor Andrew hands Gracie a napkin. "I believe between the three of us we can lay out a simple plan to help Little George with his highs and low emotional times when they hit him. I believe he's very strong mentally and with a strong will to survive. Now physically he's recovering just find and he has his youth on his side to work with."

"Now how will all of this help him get back on his feet?" Gracie ask in a choking voice.

Gazing at the stack of papers setting on his desk Doctor Andrew replies, "First off I'm a physician and not a psychologist. But I've seen sometimes just plain old common since will prevail in certain situations. Now maybe, just maybe it can work for Little George. Then on the other hand maybe not. But the one thing I do know from past experience is that by pushing someone. It's definitely not the way to go. From my point of view the best way is to let him pick his own way. Let him set his own goals."

"Ok--- Now let's just say he tries real hard and he falls flat on his face. What's plan B?" Big George ask.

Doctor Andrew nods grimly and replies, "My best guess would be to pick him up and dust him off. Encourage him to try different things. Standing by him will go miles towards his recovery. And a whole lot of patients on your part will help him too."

Gracie looks across the brown wooden desk with the glass covering at Doctor Andrew and mumbles, "I guess if he's like his grandfather and the rest the family. He's probability got a hard head and a stinking butt like a Billy Goat."

After a few minutes of laughter Doctor Andrew pauses to dab at a tear with a napkin. "Well I believe the three of us have agreed to give Little George his headway. If he stumbles, or falls we just standby and pick him up if that's what it takes to get him going again."

"Sounds like a plan Doctor Andrew. I'm with you. I just hope it works out for him," Big George says.

"All right I believe they should be about finished checking Little George out of the hospital. If you'll drive your truck around to the front of the building, I'll get one of the nurses with a wheelchair to take him out to you."

Standing up from his chair and clasping Big George's right hand and pumping it up and down Doctor Andrew says, "I wish you both the best."

CHAPTER 22

Little George is up and dressed. And his few pieces of clothing and medication are already packed.

Now all he has to do to get out of here is wait for a wheel chair and here comes his ride now.

"I bet I know a little boy who can't wait to check out of here," Nurse Applegate says as she comes into the room pushing a black wheel chair.

Sliding off the bed and plopping down onto the seat, Little George gives Nurse Applegate a big smile. "Oh you just don't know how bad I want out of here Nurse Applegate."

As the elevators doors open to the ground floor Little George happens to see Doctor Andrews out of the corner of his eye standing by the main doors of the lobby.

Little George is hoping to slide by Doctor Andrew unseen, but as his bad luck works out it didn't happen.

Doctor Andrew spots Little George coming toward the main doors.

Turning around and looking down at Little George with a deep frown on his face Doctor Andrew says, "I guess you're ready to get out of here and get back to a normal life?"

"Yes Sir. I'm more than ready," Little George replies.

As Little George watches Doctor Andrew reaches into the top pocket of his white coat and pulls out a white business card and hands it to him. "If I can ever be of service to you, please don't hesitate to call me."

Before Little George can utter a word Doctor Andrew turns and walks away.

Little George takes a moment to gaze at the card and he spies Doctor Andrew's office and home phone numbers written in black, bold, block lettering and numbers. Placing the card in his shirt pocket Little George says to no one in particular, "I guess he's in a big rush to get to his next patient,"

A soft feminine voice behind him replies, "Could be, you never know." Grandma Gracie grins sympathetically as she pushes Little George out through the hospital doors.

After being in the hospital for three months, the sudden bright sunlight gives Little George's body a sudden jolt and he feels a little dizzy for a few short seconds.

"Are you ok Little George?" Grandma Gracie ask in a concerned voice.

"I'm ok. I was so use to smelling the odors of medicines and disinfectants in the hospital. And now with all this fresh air and sunlight it may take a little time for me to get used to it again."

CHAPTER 23

As Grandma Gracie and Little George are standing in the parking lot waiting for Grandpa George to arrive. All of a sudden they hear the noise of squalling tires on the asphalt covered parking lot.

Grandma Gracie and Little George turn around and look in the direction of the noise.

To their surprise it's Grandpa George in his truck with the radio on as loud as it'll go.

Still holding on to Little George's wheel chair Grandma Gracie said, "Oh my lord... my Old Man is in his second child hood."

Slamming on the brakes and coming to a screeching stop. Grandpa George hops out the cab and looks at Gracie and Little George with surprised looks on their faces. "Hay... you folks waiting for a ride?"

"George... the people are staring at you," Grandma Gracie says with a ting of annoyance in her voice.

After Grandpa George loads up Little George's things

they head out of town.

Once on Highway Twenty Six, it's a fifteen mile drive, before getting home.

Riding in a Nineteen Fifty Five International Pickup Truck has been compared to ridding in a stage coach. For some reason it seems every bump, or pothole in the road no matter how large, or small you feel it.

After a while Grandpa George leans over the big white steering wheel and gazes in Little George's direction. "You're still hanging in there son?"

"Yes Sir. I just hope grandma makes it."

Little George is squeezed up against the passenger's side door. And Grandma Gracie is crunched in between Grandpa George and Little George.

Every time you have to shift the truck into another gear. Grandpa George has to push in on the clutch. And Grandma Gracie has to move the floor shifter into the desired gear.

Giving Grandpa George some mean eyes Grandma Gracie says, "I know one thing for certain, I'll be one happy little lady when we get home. This truck is built for two people not three."

Noticing the irritation in Grandma Gracie's voice Grandpa George decides to change the subject. "Oh... oh from the looks of my gas gage I better stop at Mittie and fill her up. Anybody need anything?"

"Yes we do. And I'm glad you asked," Grandma Gracie says. "While you're in there chewing the fat with Tom you might as well pick up a sack of flour. And a can of Blue Ribbon cane syrup. Because I feel like a dozen piping hot biscuit for supper to night should hit the spot."

No sooner are these words out of Grandma Gracie's mouth. Then a small rumbling starts to form deep down in Little George's stomach. After a second, or two it rolls up into his throat and turns into a screeching noise in his mouth.

Hearing the noise Grandma Gracie takes her eye glasses off and gives him a weird look. "If I didn't know any better. I'd think your stomach is running on empty Little George."

"I guess so. After eating that bland hospital food for two months, I believe a piece of burnt rubber would taste pretty good right now."

CHAPTER 24

After Grandpa George paid for everything and loaded back up. They headed west on Highway Twenty Six again. Three miles down the road Grandpa George turns left onto "Cherry Grove Road" where if you look to your left, or right you'll see tall pine trees. And nestled among the trees is a small white church with a small grave yard off to one side.

And a mile further down the road Grandpa George pulls the big steering wheel hard to the right. Bouncing over a wooden cattle guard and short drive down a gravel driveway sets the Acadian style home Big George and Gracie built all those many years ago. The house is perched on top a small red clay knoll and is surround by old growth long leaf pine trees and a few pecan trees.

From this vantage point the home overlooks ninety-eight acres of sandy loam soil. And in the distance you can see the emerald green forest where Flat Creek maunders through.

After Grandpa George unloads the truck he and Grandma Gracie head into the house. Little George pulls his wheel chair out of the back of the truck and plops himself down onto the seat.

Although he's been here a hundred times with his family it still feels so strange to him now. He knows that no matter how much love he'll receive here it will never replace the love he's lost.

Suddenly Little George feels two big warm hands on his shoulders and his Grandpa George's voice says, "You know your way around this place. Why don't you go in and check out your bedroom while I feed the animals."

Rolling himself through the kitchen doorway, the first thing to catch his eyes is the color of the walls. Little George remembers Grandma Gracie making a big fuss. And insisting the walls are to be painted a canary yellow with the trimming painted a glossy white.

Gazing to his left he spies Grandpa George's Franklin wood burning heater setting in a corner by a window. Seeing it brings back a favorite memory of his. He remembers the time it was cold and spitting sleet. Joy, Grandpa George, and himself ran out to the barn and dug under the straw to find the perfect sweat potatoes.

After their find they ran back to the house. After adding wood to the stove Grandpa George put the potatoes on a sheet of metal. And slide the sweet potatoes and the sheet of metal into the heater over the hot coals. Till today Little George still doesn't know why those sweat potatoes tasted, so good. He guesses it's the idea of doing something with your grandpa when you're so young.

Wheeling himself through the living room doorway Little George glances at the big brown recliner Grandpa George dozes in while pretending to be watching television. And there between the front door and the window sets

Grandma Gracie's homemade hickory rocker chair. And on the north side of the living room sets a big brownstone fire place hugging the wall.

During the winter mouths everyone would set and eat parched peanuts. And throw the hulls into the fire and watch the hulls crackle as they catch fire.

Turning to his right he rolls into his new bedroom. Little George stops for a few short minutes to let his eyes wonder about the room. Not too many years ago this was his father's bedroom. And there by the window with a set of long white curtain is his father's bed covered with a blue chenille bed cover. And next to the bed sets a night stand with a picture of Little George's father in his Fairview Panthers basketball uniform. Taking in a deep breath to his surprise he can still smell his father's scent in the room.

Now as he looks around the room his eyes start taking in the beautiful paintings hanging on the walls. Little George can remember when he was just six years old his father brought him in here and told him the story's behind each of the painting's he painted.

One of the painting hanging on the wall by the living room doorway shows a winter scene on "Flat Creek.'" The trees have lost their leaves. And the little water that's left in the creek is frozen.

As his eyes roam over the picture Little George suddenly spots a reddish brown "Fox Squirrel,'" setting on a snow covered Red Oak Tree limb holding an acorn between its two front paws. And his black eyes are staring at him.

Over on the wall by the window hangs a painting of a "Great Barn Owl.'" In the scene the owl is in a hay loaf setting on a barn rafter with his head turned around looking at you through a pair of big bright yellow penetrating eyes. Little George's daddy said every time he moved the owl would make a gurgling sound as if the owl is telling him to hurry up.

But by far Little George's favorite painting is the one his daddy did of his mother setting by a large fallen tree. She's dressed in a flowing white dress and her long beautiful auburn hair is shown cascading over her bare shoulders. And in each arm she's holding Joy and Little George at the age of two months. The landscape scene is early spring. And in the back ground you can detect a "White Dogwood Tree'" in full bloom. And next to his mother's feet you see a small wild "Azalea'" bush with its pink, and white blooms. In the back ground you see the gently sloping sandy banks of Flat Creek.

After a short minute Little George thinks to himself, "I better snap out of this reminiscing and stow my medicine in the bathroom. Then put my few pieces of clothing in the closet."

After checking everything again he decides to wheel himself out onto the back porch. From this vantage point you can look to the west and all the way down the hill to the woods. And if you stay setting long enough and the right colored clouds come drifting by at just the right time. You'll be treated to a once in a life time sunset. And after the sun has gone down and the land is dark "Mother Nature's Greats Show on Earth'" is ready to begin.

CHAPTER 25

Once the sky darkens, act one begins with the appearance of the "Evening Star"' hanging low in the eastern horizon followed by the sight of faraway galaxies with their stars blinking off and on.

After a while act two starts up right on cue. At first you think your eyes are playing a trick on you. Because it all starts out with a few tinny flashing yellow lights close to the ground. Then right before your eyes more lights start to blink on and off till it seems as though all of the trees and bushes are one big flashing yellow light. The name for this scene is "The Dance of the Fireflies."'

Now that the lights are on and the dance has begun. The only thing missing now is the orchestra and the music. With that said. Starting off slow and out of tune and after a few short minutes. The sound is building up to a crescendo of noise. And a band of thousands of cicadas began sounding off in the tree tops.

Almost mesmerized by the sights and sounds of the woods, Little George's ears pick up the sounds of faint foot falls approaching from behind him. And he hears his Grandpa George's voice saying, "Looks like the cicada bands are all tuned up and going strong tonight. Even the fireflies are putting on a great light show."

After a short few minutes Grandpa George plops down easy in his old wooden rocker chair with a cow hide stitched bottom.

Little George feels his Grandpa George's blue eyes looking at him as Grandpa George says, "Back when your daddy was a young lad. Him and old man Woodard would plant that back forty acres in "Charlestown Gray Watermelons"' and "Honeydew Cantaloupes. After the melons where ripe they would pull them and load up old Woodard's old truck and head into town. Woodard would do the driving and honking the horn. While your daddy would stick his head out the passenger's side window and yell at the top his lungs. "Sugar Town Watermelon's... Ripe and Sweet, Right Here in The Middle of the Street...Come and Get them!!"

"Did they make any money peddling that way?"

"They sure did. Why your father saved up enough money to buy that Nineteen- Fifty Chevrolet pickup truck you see parked under the barn. And with the little extra money he had left over. He bought an engagement ring for a pretty little red headed girl that lived on the other side of "Carpenters Bridge."' It was enough for your daddy at that time. And I bet you can never guess, who that red headed little girl was? And I'll give you three guesses and the first two don't even count."

"If I had to guess... I'd believe it was mother."

After a short second Little George and Grandpa George hear a voice behind them saying, "All right you two old farmers. Now that you two have solved all the great mysteries of the world and fought all the great wars. You just might want to haul your little britches in here and set down and eat some of these hot biscuits before I throw them over the fence to the hogs."

Wheeling himself in his wheel chair into the kitchen and up to a long dark brown wooden dining table, which sits in the middle of the kitchen floor. Little George remembers his daddy telling him how this table and some of the other furniture in the house came to be made.

In the late nineteen century Little George's Great Grandfather Mayo, and his brother Cyprien. Used a cross cut saw to cut down an ancient "Bald Cypress'" tree on the "Whisky Chitto Creek.'" After the tree was felled curiosity got the best of his great grandpa. It was decided they would measure this giant and count the growth rings just to find out the age of this Bald Cypress.

To everyone's surprise the tree measured one hundred and eighty feet high and better than twenty feet in circumference. And the biggest surprise was once the growth rings where counted, the tally came to five hundred and forty six years. And according to family lore two of the Cypress Knees stood over seven feet tall.

It's so quite at the table Little George can hear himself chewing and swallowing his food. All the while he's thinking. If someone walks in and yells out the three of them would keel over grave yard dead.

Finally the silence is broken by Grandpa George saying, "After the 6:00 evening news there's a barn yard burner of a basketball game coming on the T.V. between the Boston Celts and the Los Angeles Lakers. And I just happened to have a full bag of popcorn kernels and a full quirt of oil. How about it, Little George?"

Hunching both of his shoulders Little George says in a morose voice, "I think I'll call it a day a little early tonight. My leg is hurting a little."

Glancing over at his Grandpa George he spies the deep disappointment in his big blue eyes.

Little George can sense his grandparents are trying their hardest to let him know they love him and care for him. But in his heart he still can't get over the loss of his love ones, yet he is trying to live in a different environment.

"That's ok son maybe another time, when you're not so tuckered out," Grandpa George replies glumly.

Crawling under the covers and feeling like a creep Little George figures his only salvation now is to fall into a deep sleep right away.

After an hour of tossing and turning there's no such luck tonight. The only sleep he gets is bits and pieces of napes in between the rolling around and lying on his back listening to the cracking and squeaking a house makes at night.

In the quite of the darkness he can hear cars running over the gravel roads miles away.

Just about the time sleep might cover him this poor pitiful little me syndrome kicks in. "Like what in the world can a one legged sixteen year old kid do? I can definitely forget about playing basketball ever again. And running track is out of the question, or how many one legged people do you know play volleyball? While in his mind Little George thinking, "What girl in her right mind would go to a high school prom with a one legged boy?"

CHAPTER 26

"**A**re you asleep Gracie?" Big George whispers in the dark.

"No--- I've been laying here on my side in the pitch black dark waiting for you to ask me if I was asleep."

"Well---what do you think? Will Little George pull out of his down in the dump mood he's stuck in?"

"Lord... I wish I had a crystal ball to help me answer that question, but it just so happens I don't. What do you say Old Man of mine that we just leave him along? Let's just step back and let him pick his own way through his grief. I believe Doctor Andrew has a good point," Gracie says as she rolls over facing Big George.

"And pray tell me my fair Old Lady. Just what is the point?"

"It's just like Doctor Andrew said at the meeting we had with him. Let Little George set his own goals and challenges. All we need to do is stand by and cheer him on. If he stumbles and falls we pick him up and dust him off. If he wants to talk about his father, mother, or his sister we just set down with him and listen. Got that my Old Man?"

"OK... I got it Old Lady. You drive the wagon and I'll

push. I guess you know with all this talking we better get some sleep because in another two hours Sammy is going to start crowing."

"You got that right my Old Man."

CHAPTER 27

What felt like a twenty-four hour night, mercifully came to an end as Grandpa George's resident alarm clock flew up on a big oak corner post right outside Little George's bedroom window and began crowing to beat the band. Sammy is known for miles around for his capability to crow louder and longer than any rooster on Flat Creek. And this morning he is in rare form.

Little George finally has the courage to roll over and wipe the sleep from his eyes. The odor of fresh brewing chicory coffee alone with eggs and hickory smoked bacon frying in a black cast iron skillet comes whiffing under the bedroom door. Naturally this started his stomach to growling.

Lying on his back in the bed Little George pulls on a pair of his faded blue jeans. And slips on his stretched out black and gold Fairview High School tee shirt over his head. Now it's just a matter of pulling his wheel chair close enough for him to plop down onto the seat.

Coasting through the kitchen doorway Little George spies his Grandpa George seated at his usual place at the head of the table. And his Grandma Gracie is busy at the stove and has her back to him. As he pulls up to the table Little George can see his Grandpa George gazing at him from over his big white navy mug, which has the picture of the ship he served in. At the bottom of the picture in bold black lettering are the words USS JONAS INGRAM DD 938 is written.

"Well how did you sleep son?" Grandpa George ask.

Knowing how curious his Grandpa George can be. Little George simply replies, "Not too bad."

Even though his Grandma Gracie has her back to them Little George can sense she's hearing every word his Grandpa George and he are saying at the table. After a short pause Grandma Gracie ask, "How many eggs do you want Little George?"

Gazing over his shoulder Little George replies, "Two will be fine."

Coughing a few times and faking a need to clear his throat Grandpa George starts acting as if he's preparing to give a speech at the state capital building in Baton Rouge. "You know I could use a little help around the clinic. It would be like old times. What do you say?"

Getting caught off guard by Grandpa George's words Little George feels a deep burning down in his chest. After a few short seconds these words came tumbling out, "What can a one legged person do around a veterinarian clinic?"

In a split second Little George spies a look of total surprise and hurt on Grandpa George's face.

Grandpa George cast his eyes down at the table and slowly pushes his chair back. And gets up and walks to a brown wooden coat rack hanging on the wall outside the kitchen doorway.

Slipping on his coat and putting his John Deer Tractor cap on top his head. He turns and looks at Little George. "You just might be surprised at what a person can do if he tries hard enough son."

After that run in with his Grandpa George, the rest of the day Little George moped around feeling sorry for himself.

Even the farm animals turned away from him and took off running, when they spy him coming towards them.

At the end of the day this poor-poor-pitiful-little old me stuff is starting to wear a little thin. Finally Little George has to admit to himself. He's a total wreck. And it makes no since to take his frustrations out on the ones that love him unconditionally. "You little jerk."

CHAPTER 28

At the supper table tonight no one utterer's a word. The only sounds comes from a fork scrapping a plate, or a glass of milk being put down on the table. The tension is so thick you can slice through it with a butter knife.

As for Little George he's not that hungry. After he finishes his plate of corn bread and syrup with a topping of cow's cream, Little George picks up his plate and wheels over to the sink.

After placing his plate and glass in the sink. For no reason at all he decides to wheel himself out onto the front porch and watch a one of a kind "Blue Moon'" coming up over the trees.

After setting still in the dark for a few short minutes he spies a bat zigzagging through the tree tops. After a short time of gazing up into the night sky and watching the Milky Way stars gleaming. A sudden rush of emotions comes rushing up into his chest and tears start welling up in his eyes.

Trying with all his might to suppress these feelings they come tumbling out anyway. What feels like an eternity finally ends as he watches his tears falling onto the porch flooring and making little wet dimples.

As Little George's sobbing starts to subside. He feels two warm hands resting on his shoulders.

Unknown to him at the time his Grandpa George is standing in the shadows watching over him. Gently squeezing Little George's shoulders Grandpa George ask softly, "Are you trying to find haven up there among all those stars?"

"I think so. Do you believe that time helps heals the hurt Grandpa?" Little George says as he wipes a tear with his shirt sleeve.

Little George can see his Grandpa George raise his head up and gaze up at the night sky. Then he runs his hand over a three day growth of salt and peppered beard. "Seems like the old folks would say that from time to time, but I'm not so sure it works that way. I believe you can never repair a broken heart. The hurt stays with you all of your days. But as time goes on it doesn't seem to hurt as bad."

After his Grandpa George removes his hands from his shoulders, Little George gazes up into his face. As his Grandpa George turns to walk away. He spies a silvery streak of moisture running down the side of his Grandpa's cheek.

CHAPTER 29

Pulling the bed covers up under his chin and stacking both pillows under his head Little George reaches over and pulls the window shade up.

The moon's reflection on the polished wooden floor cast the room in an ire glow. It also gives his daddy's paintings a life of their own.

The big Fox Squirrel up in the tree munching on a big brown juicy acorn seems to be moving its mouth, as if he's chewing.

Even the big Barn Owl setting on a rafter is blinking his big yellow eyes at him.

As he lets his eyes wonder over to the painting of his mother holding Joy and him. To his amazement the first thing to catch his eyes is the glow in her long auburn hair. This makes Little George start to wonder how on earth did his daddy accomplish this scene, or is it just an optical illusion, because no one can paint this type of glow in someone's hair.

In a few minutes time his eyes lids feel like they weigh a ton. After falling into a deep sleep at times in his dreaming, Little George can hear voices echoing in the distance, yet at times the voices come rushing up to his side.

To his complete surprise all at once he recognizes the voices of his love ones. But in his frustration he can't see their faces, or their body's.

But he keeps waving his arms frantically and calling out their names and even trying to touch them. Then all at once in a hazy gray cloud their voices disappear into nothing.

Suddenly out of nowhere a loud booming clap of thunder snaps Little George out of his dreaming. The house shakes and another clap of thunder rolls across the coal black night sky.

As Little George opens his eyes he spies the window is still open and a fine misty rain is blowing in. As he reaches out to close the window shut he spies a strike of blue, white lighting racing across the night sky lighting the black night outside like day.

After closing the window, and pulling the sheet up to his neck. Little George glances at the silver colored "Big Ben"' alarm clock, on the night stand by his father's picture. He notices the luminous hands are showing 4:15. Setting bolt up straight in the bed and running his hand through his unruly red hair he starts thinking. "Man... where did the night go?"

Little George knows in another thirty minutes his grandparent's feet's will hit the floor and another day will begin on Flat Creek. So this gives him plenty of time to decide which direction he wants the rest of his life to go.

As he see his life right now. The eases way out would be the one he is on now. It's call, "the set on your butt and moan the blues routine."' The only problem with this routine is. No one seems to be paying any attention to him. And he's sure his parents wouldn't be proud of him doing this.

On the other hand he does have another choice. This one is called. "Get off your butt and get on with your life right now routine'"

CHAPTER 30

After rolling out of bed and jumping onto his wheel chair, Little George races into the bathroom and performs his famous three minute routine for getting ready for the day.

The first part of his routine is to brush your teeth. Then run a comb through your hair. And the most important hygiene act of all is called the Splash a hand full of cold water into your sleepy face and wipe dry.

Now it's just a matter of finding you're cleanest dirty clothes to put on. And you're ready to face the world head on.

After doing all this, Little George pulls up to the kitchen table with a big smile on his face. Gazing at his Grandpa George he says, "Good Morning. And how did you sleep?"

Hearing Little George saying these words almost causes his Grandpa George to drop his big navy mug full of piping hot coffee onto his lap.

Then his Grandpa George commences coughing and choking. And the color of his face goes from crimson to a deep purplish color of an Eggplant. And Little George also notices tears welling up in his eyes.

Lucky Grandma Gracie hears all the commotion at the table. She drops her stainless steel spatula on the floor. And runs over to Grandpa George and gives him a couple of hand slaps between the shoulder blades.

Finally catching his breath after a few seconds his color starts returning to normal. And Grandpa George seems to settle down a little.

Although he and Grandma Gracie still have this dazed and confused look on their faces.

Grandpa George is the first to recover. "By...Golly you must have got up on the wrong side of the bed this morning Little George."

Giving his Grandpa George his best Deer-In-The-Headlights look Little George says, "I'm Ok grandpa. It's just I'm excited to start the day off."

Sliding his chair back far enough to reach into the back pocket of his pants, Grandpa George pulls out a faded red handkerchief and commence to dabbing at the tears in the corner of his eyes.

After a short time with a big grin on his face Grandpa George stands up from the table and looks at Grandma Gracie. "Well Gracie it's time for me and my assistant to head out and check on our patents."

Going down the same gravel road where not more than three months ago, Little George loss his loved ones makes a cold chill run up his spine.

As the truck approaches the Flat Creek Bridge, Little George turns his head and closes his eyes.

Without thinking Grandpa George says, "You know it looks like this year just might be a good year for water melons."

Opening his eyes Little George says, "Huh."

Glancing at Little George out of the corner of his eye

Grandpa George says, "Your mind must be a thousand miles away."

CHAPTER 31

If you were to paint a picture of Grandpa George's veterinarian clinic it would show a late nineteen century barn made entirely out of cypress wood. The main parts of the barn are painted a country blue and the trimming painted a glossy white.

The roof is all wooden singles and perched on top of the roof sit's a "Widowers Walk'" with a light that shines twenty-four hours a day-seven days a week.

When you walk up to the two big wooden front door you'll notice hanging on either side of the massive doors the two big brass lights. One has a dark green light in it and the other has a blood red light. When Little George asked his Grandpa George about these lights he says, "They show you which way you're going. Red is for left and green is for right."

At 7:30 a.m. sharp Grandpa George inserts his big brass key into the front door lock. As soon as he gives the door a slight nudge with his shoulder. The hinges supporting the door make a slight squeaking noise. All at once you can hear a chorus of howling, barking, and meowing coming from the back room of the building.

Gazing down at Little George from over the top of his Ben Franklin glasses, Grandpa George says, "It sounds like our patients are glade you and I are here. I'll tell you what. I'll start mixing the cat and dog food while you clean and refill the water bowls. This way we can get the show on the road."

CHAPTER 32

As the day wears on the clinic settles into a normal everyday routine. People start coming in with their pets for checkups and vaccine shots.

Uncle Bill and Grandpa George are busy checking a dozen head of cattle for Bangs. They've even had a few dogs, and cats, which were in need of a dip for tick's, and fleas. The only exciting thing to happen all day is, when Little George flipped his wheel chair over trying to catch an escaped cat who figured out it could slid its skinny front paw through the cage bars and flip the outside latch up thereby gaining his freedom.

As lunch time approaches, Little George decides to take his brown bag and eat his fried egg sandwich his Grandma Gracie made for him into his Grandpa George's office.

Setting in his Grandpa's big black plush office chair gives him a since of importance. Looking at the teal green colored walls Little George counts a dozen pictures of ducks and geese in flight.

And a few pictures show different breeds of championship dogs in varies stages of poses.

Looking behind him hanging on the wall is Little George's favorite picture. It's a portrait showing his mother standing next to his daddy, and his Grandpa George, and Grandma Gracie holdings hands. And in front Joy, and Little George are setting on the ground.

Wadding up the wax paper his egg sandwich was wrapped with and stuffing it into the brown bag. Little George decides to cock Grandpa George's big chair back as far as it can go and take a short nap. But before he can close his eyes he notices the shiny black phone setting on the desk at arm's length.

He remembers what Doctor Andrew said about calling him if he needed help. Twisting onto his side Little George pulls his wallet out of his back pocket. After a few short seconds of digging in his wallet he finds the card Doctor Andrews gave him when he left the hospital. Holding the card at arm's length and gazing at the card. Little George thinks. "Why not call him."

He reaches over and picks up the black receiver and cradles it in his hand. Using his other hand Little George begins to use the rotor dial to call the number for Doctor Andrew's office. All the while he is thinking. "He's probably busy, or not even there."

On the second ring a voice on the other end of the line said, "Doctor Andrew's office... how can I help you?"

Getting caught by surprise Little George stammers, "Hello Doctor Andrew this is Little George. How are you doing?"

"Oh... this is a surprise. And I'm doing just find. How about you?"

"I'm doing just great Doctor Andrew. I know you're busy. So I'll get to the reason for the call. I'm wondering if the prosthetic leg is still available."

"Why yes it is,"

"That's fantastic. I've been thinking about giving it another try. I know now there's a lot of stuff I can't do setting in a wheel chair."

"Well... now that's the best news I've heard in a long time. I'll tell you what I can do. Just give me a couple of hours. And I'll have someone deliver the leg to your grandparent's home on Flat Creek."

"That would be great Doctor Andrew. Thanks a lot."

"Now before we hang up, I'd like to ask you how are you're grandparent's doing? And what on earth is all that barking in the back ground about?"

Laughing Little George replies, "The answer to the first part of your question is. They are both doing fine. Considering the fact they're putting up with me. And the answer to part two of your question is. I'm now helping grandpa at the clinic and the barking is coming from our customers complaining about the service."

After giving his answers there's a moment of silence at the other end of the phone line. "Are you still there Doctor Andrew?"

"Yes...yes I am still here. I'm glad things are working out for you. And if I can be of help to you give me a call."

"I will. And thanks for everything."

After a moment of silence the line goes dead. And Little George replaces the receiver back in its cradle.

Scratching his head Little George stares at the phone for a time. As he's getting back into his wheel chair his Grandpa George comes walking through the doorway with a big grin on his face. "I see you've been working on the books."

"Close, but no cigar... I was talking to Doctor Andrew about sending me the prosthetic leg for me to tryout again. I don't seem to be doing a very good job by seating in this wheel chair."

A surprised look slowly spreads across his Grandpa George's face and his brow furrows as he says, "By-Golly there's no doubt in my mind you can do it. Come on let's tell everyone to tighten up around here so we can close up a little early and go home and tell the good news to your grandmother."

CHAPTER 33

As Grandpa George and Little George are turning off the lights in the clinic. Little George hears the screeching sounds of tires on the concrete parking lot outside. As he wheels himself up to the front door to see what's going on. A tall man with dark beady eyes and a disheveled look comes busting through the front door carrying a dark brown dirt covered bloody bundle in his arms.

The man rushes up to Grandpa George and in a winded voice, "Mr. ... can you please help me? Someone just ran over this dog and left it to die in the ditch out by "Old Hoy.""

As Grandpa George reaches out to take the dog from the stranger. The dog lets out a soft whimper.

Eying the stranger with a critical eye Grandpa George says in a skeptical tone, "Well now... I don't really know what I can do for the dog till I get some X Rays. Then I can see what damage has been done."

Grandpa George turns to Little George and ask, "You feel up to helping me?"

After an hour of complicated and tedious work Grandpa George gazes over the operation table. "We've done all we can do. Now it's up to the good lord."

He picks up the dog from the table and carries it to a special cage for the night. In his heart Little George knows his Grandpa tried with all his knowledge to save the dog's left hind leg. But in the end he had to amputate it to save her life.

From the look in his Grandpa George's eyes Little George can tell he's not a happy camper. "You know Little George I've got a few questions to ask that stranger. Because in all my years as a Doctor of Veterinarian Medicine. Never have I seen an animal get run over and end up with twelve gage double 00 buck shot in it."

"Maybe the man who brought her in can fill in the missing pieces of the puzzle?"

As they come into the reception area they both spy the front door standing wide open and not a soul is in sight. Little George can tell by the way his Grandpa is standing in the doorway clenching his big hands then unclenching them it might have been a good idea for the stranger to disappear.

Turning around and gazing at Little George and rubbing the back of his neck Grandpa George dead panned, "I guess we might as well get cleaned up. I might just take a ride out to Old Hoy in a couple of days and do a little snooping around."

CHAPTER 34

Little George is finishing up stacking the clean towels in the operating room and putting the dirty, blood covered ones in the dirty bin to be picked up later.

All this time he's thinking about this dog and the way she was abused. It also has him wondering what her breed might be. Although she's not a big dog she has strong legs and a beautiful wavy mahogany colored coat. Hearing foot falls behind him Little George is thinking to himself. "Here comes the answer to my questions."

"Do you know what breed the brown Gyp might be Grandpa?"

Looking up at the ceiling and scratching the back of his neck Grandpa George replies, "I'm not one hundred percent sure. But if I had to lay my money down I'd say she's what duck hunters call a Chesapeake-Bay-Retriever.

Now the reason I say that is back some years back Mr. Willie and I took off on a little duck hunting trip to Grand Chenier. Our guide had a dog that looks just like that Gyp. And when I asked him, "What breed is your dog?" He said, "She's a Chesapeake Bay Retriever."

Squirming around in his wheel chair and squinting his eyes Little George asked in an anxious voice, "Let's just say nobody comes in and claims her for their own. What are the chances of me keeping her for my own?"

Grandpa George looks down at Little George from over the tops of his Ben Franklin eye glasses, which are perched on the end of his nose. "Hum... let me think here now. I don't know of any laws that says you can't keep her. After all she doesn't have a collar, or a dog tag. So I don't see why you can't keep her. After all you both have a lot in common."

With a surprise look on his face Little George says, "And how can that possible be?"

"Well this is how I got this figured out. Both you and the dog can do Math," Grandpa George says with a chuckle in his voice.

Rolling his eyes in his head Little George replies, "Ok I'll bit. How can the dog and I do Math?"

"Why...By...Golly, the dog puts down three legs and carries one. And you put down one leg and carry one. That's how."

After their laughing finally starts to subside a little, both Grandpa George and Little George are now using towels to dab at the tears of laughter, which keeps welling up in their eyes.

Even on the ride home Grandpa George has to pull over to the side of the road. And dab at his eyes and wipe his glasses to see. By the time they reach home their sides are aching from all the laughing.

Walking through the kitchen doorway Grandma Gracie

gives them her once over stare. "From the looks of you two "Knot Heads"' red eyes a person might think you two been out on "Whisky Chitto Creek"' visiting old man Noah's Moonshine Still."

"It's not quiet that bad," Grandpa George replies.

Looking up at his Grandma Gracie and shrugging his shoulders Little George says, "I talked to Doctor Andrew this afternoon and he said he would send the prosthetic leg out to me."

"You must have put a bug in Doctor Andrew's ear. Because a young man just dropped off a package for you and he laid it on your bed."

Wheeling himself up to the side of his bed Little George reaches out and starts opening the package.

After struggling to open the package, it dawns on Little George someone must have a grudge against him, because there must be at least a mile of tape holding the package together. After ten minutes of cutting and hacking with his "Case"' pocket knife he finally has this monster of a package opened up and there it is. The one thing that will help him be his old self again.

The first thing he has to do is pull the rubber stocking up over his stump. And pull as hard as he can on the prosthetic leg to get it over the rubber stocking. Now the fun part begins. As he reaches out and grabs a hand hold on the headboard of the bed.

The hardest part is going to be pulling himself up into a standing position, because for a few short second he will feel a little light headed.

Knowing he can't walk on the hard wood flooring with just the plastic leg. Little George finds his right foot tennis shoe and slips it over the prosthetic foot.

Now he's off to see how many pieces of furniture, or bones he can break. Holding on to the wall while he take's little baby steps seems to be working for him at this time.

Now he's through the living room doorway. And slowly works himself around the Television set, then around the fire place. Three more steps to go and he's leaning up against the kitchen door jamb with his hands on his hips and saying, "Anyone in here want to run a foot race?"

CHAPTER 35

This morning Little George waddles over to the kitchen table and sets down to a big bowl of coffee milk and crumbled up corn bread left over from the night before.

The only problem he's having right now is his Grandpa George's eyes are trying to bore a hole into the side of his head. Little George has a feeling when his Grandpa can't stand him eating and ignoring him at the same time. He'll break down and say what's bugging him.

After a few fake dry coughs and a fake sip from his empty mug of coffee Grandpa George says in a skeptical voice, "I know I'm getting a little old. But would you mind humoring your old grandpa by telling me why on god's green earth would you want a retriever out here in these piney woods, when all we have are Whitetail Deer, Fox, and Cat Squirrels. And a bunch of Swamp Rabbits, and Cotton Tail Rabbits mixed in with a few Raccoons, and Armadillos to boot."

Slowly whipping his mouth with a napkin and gazing at his grandpa Little George replies, "I've been thinking about training her for a run at the Grand-Nite-Championship."

Upon hearing these words a fit of spitting, and sputtering starts, because his Grandpa George was taking a bit of corn bread.

Getting up from the table Grandpa George mutters anxiously, "It's a little too early in the day for this. Why who ever heard of someone taking a duck dog and training it to tree Raccoons." And out the back door he went.

Looking over his shoulder Little George hears his Grandma Gracie say, "Well the good thing about all of this is. You got your grandpa's blood pressure up."

CHAPTER 36

Early spring in southwest Louisiana is a sight to behold, especially, when you take a slow walk in the woods.

You just might spot a White Dogwood in full bloom, or maybe a Wild Azalea bush in all its glory.

And if you happen to find a log to sit down on and you don't move a muscle for a while. You just might see the new born baby animal's scurrying across the forest floor, or the hustle and bustle of the parents trying to satisfy their babies never ending hunger.

If you look closely at the trees you can see an emerald green coloring starting to show and the odor of fresh plowed fields fill the air.

After Little George walks a short distance on the east bank of Flat Creek. He spies the place where his daddy painted the picture of his mother holding Joy and him in her arms.

Looking at the oaks and pine trees he can tell by the length of their shadows on the ground late evening is approaching.

Crossing over Flat Creek by walking on a fallen tree log, Little George finds what he's looking for.

It's an old cattle trail of long ago that the old folks would tell stories about how the early settlers and Indians used this trail for trading and hunting.

As he's walking along the trail he starts thinking about how he got the name Little George and Grandpa is called Big

George and his daddy was George Junior. So that left Little George with

George James the Third, or like his Grandma Gracie said, "Little George will do him just fine."

Climbing up on a big red oak corner post and flipping one leg over the top of the barbwire fence and climbing over the other side of the fence.

Little George starts walking out of the woods and into a cattle lane which leads up the hill to his grandparent's home.

As he's walking along Little George feels he's making some progress on handling his mood swings.

All because he now has a beautiful dog he named Lady. And he's also back in school with all his classmate and walking on his prosthetic leg full time. This has helped a great deal. Also in a few weeks he's going to do the impossible. He'll start trying to train a Chesapeake Bay retriever to tree raccoons and win the Grand-Nite-Championship.

CHAPTER 37

N ow that he's back ridding the school bus Little George has started being a people watcher and listener.

His favorite person to watch and listen to is Mr. Mack his school bus driver. Mr. Mack has a thin built. And Little George has never seen him wear anything but "Liberty'" blue overalls with a red tin Prince Albert tobacco can in the top pocket of his overalls. He also wears a brown Stetson felt hat perched on top a head full of unruly salt and pepper colored hair. But his warm demeanor and love of telling stories of how it was, when he was their age growing up is what gets to your heart. He can remember the times before there was electricity, or telephones lines running in the Flat Creek community.

It was a time, when folks would come and visit each other in the late evenings and sit on the front porch and talk for hours.

And the long hot summer days spent in the fields hoeing and pulling corn, or cutting hay. And at the end of the day as the sun is setting, Mr. Mack and his brothers would run down and jump into the cool water of Flat Creek and lay there and let the water run over their hot, tired bodies.

Or the stories of the cold winter months and the time spent looking for rich lighter pine knots to help start a warm fire in the fireplace. So you could get up and get dressed on a cold windy mourning.

And how everyone in the community would come over and help you butcher hogs. And at the end of a story he would slap his knee with his big callous hand and look you in the eye. "Those where the good old days boys and I hope they never come back."

CHAPTER 38

With the arrival of October Lady and Little George spend every minute they can in the woods. The hardest part about training her is to keep her attention on the job at hand. When a Quail whistles her ears go straight up and she turns and looks in the direction of the whistle. Or a squirrel barks at another squirrel and her eyes follow the noise. And she cocks her head sideways as if she is trying to figure out what's this all about.

Little George knows if she can get her use to the noises of the woods he can start her on a training routine. But right now patent's is golden and the last thing he wants to do is break her spirit by hollering and fussing at her.

After jumping off the bus at his grandpa's clinic Little George heads for the back door. Before he can say "Hi" Lady's is already coming his way with her tail banging the sides of the cages.

After a good brush down it's time to hit the woods and get some training in before dark. As he's filling his old dented canteen with drinking water a familiar voice behind him says, "With all that barking going on I figured you might be back here with Lady. I brought you a little something that might help you out with training her."

Turning around to see what his Grandpa George has in his hands Little George immediately recognizes his father's cow horn hanging in his big hand.

It's the one his father used, when he won the Grand-Nite-Championship. All of a sudden Little George feels a stinging sensation building up behind his eyes. He takes a big swallow and reaches out his hand.

Not in a million years could he ever see himself holding something his father had cherished so much. "Do you think I'll be able to blow it like daddy?" Little George ask with a cracking voice.

"Why there's no doubt in my mind you will. With a little practice Lady will know what you want her to do just by you blowing on this horn."

CHAPTER 39

As crunch time nears Lady and Little George spend more time in the woods. Even on weekends, it's in the woods at 7:00 a.m. then out at 10:00 p.m. And on school days they hit the woods at 7:00 p.m. and out at 10:00 p.m.

With all the training under her belt Ladies picked up on Little George's voice commands and his cow horn signal's.

But the only problem with too much training is eventually it begins to take a toll on you and your dog. Running in the woods on a pitch black night with only a head light on your head and a battery clipped to your belt for you to see where you're going. And to keep you from falling into old stump holes left over from the days of blowing up rich pine stumps to make turpentine.

Or the worst is tripping over vines and old blow down trees and brier patches, which maunder throughout the woods. And running up and down the sandy banks of Flat Creek till at times you feel like one large red scratch.

There are times when Lady and Little George are so tuckered out that all they can do is lay on the ground. And look up at the bright stars of the Milky Way.

After a short few minutes they roll over and get up off the

ground. And drag their tired worn out butts under the fence. And start their long walk up the hill toward home.

Once there it doesn't mean the day is done for Little George. He'll spend another thirty minutes, or more picking dog and seed ticks off both himself and Lady.

After the tick picking is over. It's time to feed and water Lady, and find something for himself to eat. After a few bits of food he'll fill the bath tub with hot water and soak till he's almost water logged.

Now he's ready for some shut eye. And of course all this has to be done without waking his grandparents from their sleep. The only advantage he has going for him is the snoring and mumbling coming from their bedroom.

CHAPTER 40

With Sammy making his announcement that the sun has resin. Little George jumps out of bed and gets busy getting dressed.

Last night while he was eating a bowl of toast bread and milk Little George spied a big brown envelop setting in the middle of the kitchen table.

But with the lights off and not wanting to turn them on he left it along. Now this morning the lights are on and from what he can see it says, To Mr. George the 3rd" in big black block lettering and on the top left it reads, "From the Grand-Nite-Championship Council.'"

Little George reaches over to picks up the brown envelope off the table. And his hands start to tremble and his knees feel weak.

Standing in one spot and just looking down at his name on something he's been dreaming about for a long time.

His Grandma Gracie's soft voice jolts him as she says, "Why don't you go ahead and open it up instead of standing there trying to stair a hole in it."

For some reason trying to open an envelope, which is sealed with some kind of super glue is hard enough. But, when all of your fingers have turned into thumbs, it makes it almost impossible to do. "Here Little George hand it to me before you hurt yourself," Grandpa George says as he walks in through the kitchen doorway.

Reaching into the front pocket of his overalls and pulling out his "Old Timer'" pocket knife and opening the big blade. Grandpa George slides the point under the flap of the envelope and slides the blade from one end to the other. Grandpa George hands the open envelope back to Little George. "Here you go young man."

Sliding the paper content of the envelope out Little George's eyes grow bigger and bigger as he reads the first page. Which is typed in bold black lettering.

After a short while Little George says in an excited voice, "Man this is what I've been waiting a long time for."

"Now that your eyes have popped out of their sockets and you have that Jackass Eating Briars Grin on your face. Maybe you can let your old grandpa and grandma in on your little secret," Grandpa George says.

Looking up from the slip of paper in his hand Little George says "Oh...Ya!! The first page is a welcome letter with an invitation for me to participate in the Grand-Nite-Championship Tryouts. And the second page is the rules of the tryouts and how many Timers and Counters there will be. Also they have the points, which will be given to the ones who place all the way from first place to fourth place. And the last page is the starting times and the places and dates the tryouts will be held."

"Sounds pretty good to me, but where are these tryouts going to be held?" Big George ask.

"Let's see...the first tryout is at" Sugar Town"" on January the twelfth and the start time is 7:00 p.m.

And the second one is at the "Soap Stone Community'" on January the nineteenth and starting at 7:00 p.m.

After that one it's off to "Mittie'" on January the twenty six and again starting time is 7:00 p.m.

After those three tryouts it seems we have a week off to get ready for the Grand-Nite-Championship at "Grant'" on February the ninth. And it also starts at 7:00 p.m. And for some reason we meet behind the Old Gym at "Fairview High School.'"

Scratching an itch behind his right ear Big George says, "Umm…humm. Seems to me there's some rough country around some of those places you just named. Why I imagine there are some places a man has never walked. And that brings me to my next subject."

"And just what might that be?" Grandma Gracie ask.

Big George walks over to the kitchen table and pulls out his chair and plops down on it. Grandpa George shifts his gaze first at Little George then his wife. And after a short few seconds in a solemn voice, "On my way to the clinic yesterday morning I spied a little skinny raccoon walking on the side of the road with a tinny bundle tied to a stick hanging over his shoulders. And when I passed him I noticed he had a cardboard sign hanging around his neck that reads, "Moving out of Flat Creek."

After their sides quit aching Little George ask, "Wonder why it would say that?"

"Will I believe it's because every raccoon on Flat Creek has been treed at least four times in the last three months," Big George says dabbing at a tear on his cheek.

CHAPTER 41

Saturday morning starts out bright and early. Even before Sammy has a chance to do his morning crowing Little George is up and dressed.

Walking in through the kitchen doorway Little George spies his Grandma Gracie's hot water kettle setting on the white gas stove. It's letting a small amount of steam escape out its spout. He knows from past experience in a few seconds it will begin a high pitch whistling noise. And his Grandma will pick it up and pour the hot water over the coffee grinds, which are in the tall silver coffee pot. After a few minutes the water will turn into a strong black coffee brew.

Setting at the kitchen table with both elbows resting on the top and gazing at Little George with a critical eye his Grandpa George says, "Boy you look like nine hundred miles of bad road. A little more and you'd look like one big continuance scratch."

Digging around on his plate of fried eggs and hickory smoked ham with his fork Little George replies in a tired voice, "I guess with all this training and going to school it's about to wear my out."

Hearing these words coming from her grandson Gracie says, "You know what you need Little George? You need someone to help you out. A person that's not scared of the woods at night…that's what you need By-Golly."

Looking around at his grandmother Little George says in a tired voice, "I whole heartily agree with you grandma. But, who is the question?"

Standing in the middle of the kitchen and watching his Grandma Gracie's body movement. Little George can tell her mind is racing like a runaway nuclear reactor.

After pacing the floor for a few short minutes a big smile spreads across Grandma Gracie face as she says, "I think I know just the person, who can help you and Lady win the Grand-Nite-Championship."

Getting caught off guard by this remark Little George stammers, "Who can that be?"

"Judy Long that's, who. Why that girl can run through the woods like a deer and she keeps those three "Jug Headed'" brothers of hers inline. Come to think about it you're both in the same grade at school and you both work after school at your grandpa's clinic."

With a blown away expression on his face Little George blurts out, "But she's a girl."

"Well now…By…Golly you did notice that. Why, who in heavens name do you think helped your daddy win his Grand-Nite-Championship young man?"

As Little George gazes up at, the white tin stamped ceiling of the kitchen while trying hard to come up with something real cute to answer his grandma back with. He notices out of the corner of his eye Grandma Gracie picked up a wet dish cloth. So to save face he mumbles, "I give up. Who was it?"

Looking at Little George through her hazel eyes and

one hand on her hip and the other holding the wet wash cloth Grandma Gracie says, "Why... it was your mother, who helped him. She's the one, who gave up her free time to do it when no one else would."

Little George knows in an instant he has this stupid kid look on his face as he replies back, "I sure didn't know that."

CHAPTER 42

The only good thing about today is its Halloween Night. And it's a good bet once the animals are feed and watered Big George will likely close the clinic a little early. Because everyone in the state of Louisiana and Mississippi knows what happens on Halloween Night.

Yep…you guessed it. L.S.U. and the Ole Miss Rebels play football. And this year they play in Baton Rouge. And the only way Big George will miss this game will be if he is in a horizontal position at the morgue.

Walking through the living room on his way to his bed room with his mind on how in the world is he going to ask Judy for her help in training Lady. When out of no where's this booming voice interrupts Little George's thinking by saying, "Where on earth are you going. I've already gone outside and turned the T.V. antenna towards Baton Rouge. In a few minutes they're going to kick the ball."

Glancing over his shoulder Little George says, "No football for this kid tonight. I have some serious planning to do."

Hearing this remark coming from Little George set his Grandpa George off like a Brahma Bull tangled up in a Barbwire fence. "My lord it's still a good thirty minutes till sunset. Why the chickens haven't even got up on their roost for the night yet. What on earth is this world coming to?"

The one thing Little George learned at an early age about his grandpa is. It's best not to fall into one of his traps. And tonight his Grandpa George is in one of his better arguing moods. So no matter what he'll say. Little George will automatically lose this argument.

Lying on his side facing the window, Little George can see a big orange harvest moon casting a burnt glow of light over the tree tops. Knowing in a few months Lady and he will be competing with some of the best raccoon dogs in the world makes it even a greater challenge for him to ask Judy for her help. Pulling the covers up over his head he knows tonight is going to be another long and restless night.

CHAPTER 43

Little George spent all day Sunday dodging his Grandpa George. And now Monday has finally arrived. All day at school Little George avoided Judy. But now school is out. And it's now, or never for him. As he hops off the school bus he heads for the back door of the clinic. But a loud and booming voice stops him dead in his tracks, "Boy you sure missed a great game Saturday night. Those Tigers and Rebels wore each other out," Grandpa George hollers out.

Glancing over his shoulder in the direction of his Grandpa George's voice Little George spies Mr. Phil and his Grandpa George in the barn yard checking the hooves of a young black and white paint colt. "Why are you in such a big hurry?" Grandpa George shouts out.

Waving his arm in the air Little George shouts back, "Not now. I got some very important business to take care of."

Little George spent all weekend trying to come up with a clever way to ask Judy for her help. He knows he's used up at least one hundred pages of paper writing down all the neat ways to ask a person for help he knows of.

After reading them all, he threw the papers away he'd spent all his time writing words and sentences on. Because all of this time he was trying to impress Judy.

Walking in through the back door he suddenly gets the idea of simply ask her for her help. After all what can she say? Yes she will, or No she can't.

Looking around the cages his Grandpa George keeps the dogs and cats in. He spots Judy in a far off corner of the room. It's the part of the room where grandpa keeps the most critical animals. And Judy is bent over feeding a sick puppy. She has on a green surgical smock with her long auburn hair put up in a ponytail.

As soon as Lady senses his presences, she comes running up to him with her tail slapping the sides of the shiny stainless steel cages. Turning around to see where Ladies gone Judy says, "I had a hunch it was you by the way she took off."

Standing there rooted to the concrete floor like a tree with both hands starting to moisten Little George stammers, "I guess you heard I'm trying to train Lady for a run at the Grand-Nite-Championship."

With a hint of amusement in her bluish green eyes Judy replies, "I heard a little something about that."

Gazing down at his dust covered tennis shoes and trying to clear his throat. After a few short seconds Little George says, "Well I've run into a little bit of a problem. With everything that needs to be done while you're running through the woods training a dog. You just can't do it all by yourself. Because first off you have to keep the time your dog treed and the time you spotted the raccoon. And you have to holler out, "I got a Tree over here."

After all of that is done. You still have to keep count of how many times you're dog treed. And the biggest problem is you have to do all this while you have a head light perched on top your head. And a stop watch around your neck. And you also have a cow horn slung over your shoulder and a clip board in one hand and a pencil in the other."

All this time Judy is wiping her hands on a white towel and gazing at Little George. And with a surprised look on her face. "My... I didn't know it was such a complicated process to train a dog to tree."

"It is believe you me. But what I'm trying to ask you is. Would you be my assistant and help me train Lady?"

At first Little George spies Judy's brow furrowing as she stands on one foot and then the other foot. And all this time she's staring at a small spot on the unfinished concrete floor. After a few short minute she places one finger under her chin and looks him in the eyes and says, "I might be able to help you. But first I have to ask my daddy."

Feeling a little light headed and dizzy Little George chokes out, "Ok."

CHAPTER 44

The last three weeks of training have been a blur for Little George and Judy. The new schedule Little George wrote up for Judy and himself doesn't give them much free time. On school days Little George has to limit their time in the woods, because Judy and he have home work to do. So he figures if they hit the woods at 6:00 p.m. after their work at his Grandpa George's clinic is done. Then wrap things up at 9:00 p.m. That gives Judy and him three hours of training time. Then, when Saturday roll's around they can hit the woods at the crack of dawn and come out at sunset. As for Sunday they can be in the woods training right after church is over. After a little training time they can take a break in the woods and go over their reports and check on Lady's progress.

"I don't see how we can improve her training any more then what she's doing now Little George," Judy said while putting her hair up into a ponytail.

"I think your right. It's time we pack it up and head up the hill for home."

CHAPTER 45

L ittle George and Judy are walking on an old cow trail that leads up the north side of the hill which Little George's grandparent's house sets on.

Usually Lady runs ahead of Judy and Little George. And most of the time she'll scare up a cotton tail rabbit, or a slow moving opossum. But this evening she is acting like she is ready for her brush down and a big bowl of food with water. Every once in a while she stops and looks behind herself as if she is checking on Judy and Little George.

Spotting Lady's odd behaver Judy says, "I guess we better walk a little faster, or we'll lose her,"

"I believe she's more than ready for the house."

As they pass under the hay loft of the barn Little George hears Grandpa George's voice calling from the feed room, "Hold up there Little George. I got a little information for you."

Little George says goodbye to Judy then turns and climbs up the wooden steps, which leads into the feed room. Once there he finds Grandpa George setting in a pile of dried corn shucks. "Need a little help?" Little George ask.

"Nope---I'm just wrapping up. Do you remember me telling you a couple of weeks back I was planning on taking a little ride out to Old Hoy and do a little snooping around. And how that stranger lied to us about how Lady got hurt."

"Yes Sir I remember."

With a big grin showing on his face Grandpa George says, "Well I got the chance to take a little drive out to where you turn off Highway Twenty Six onto the old dirt road, which leads you back into Old Hoy. And right off the bat I found where it looks like a struggle took place in a ditch. When I got out to take a good look I spied some old dried up blood and where something tore up the side of the ditch."

Looking at his Grandpa George through hurt eyes Little George ask, "But why would someone just shoot a dog?"

"I don't know. But I believe there's some "Knot Heads"' that are trying real hard to hide something they're doing back in Old Hoy. So I figured while I was out there I'd do a little creeping around and see what I might find."

"Did you find anything?" Little George ask in an anxious voice.

"Oh...You might say I did. From what I seen out there it seems like an awful lot of traffic is going in and out of that place. And usually that's a sign that something is going on in a place, which has nothing but miles and miles of prairie grass. And every once in a while a little hard wood timber stands that's left over from the big timber cutting days of long ago."

"That's weird. What can you do out there?"

"That's just it. After finding those tire tracks I decided to drive a little further down the road. As I got to the big concrete blocks where the old water tower once stood that held the big water tank they used to fill the coal fired steam engines with. All of a sudden I hear a truck engine start up and leave in a hurry and shortly after the sound of a gun going off."

"Somebody shot at you?" Little George says with excitement showing in his eyes.

"I'm not sure if they fired the gun up in the air to scare me away. But whichever way it was done it worked. I got out of there as fast as I could. And when I got home last night I called Sheriff Thomas and told him what I'd found and what I'd run into."

"What does he think is going on out there?"

"He hasn't a glue. But he did tell me an interesting little story about how the law folks here in Louisiana and Texas are having a big problem trying to catch a big marijuana drug smuggling ring."

"Do they think they come from around here?"

"They don't know for sure Little George. But the sheriff did say one thing that sounded a little odd."

"I'm all ears," Little George replies.

"Well… he said for some reason they always lose the drug smugglers, when they head back east out of Texas. Because there's so many little country dirt and gravel roads that leads you around at least a dozen little settlements and one red light towns. It would take an Army to track these crooks down."

"The only thing I know there aren't many people in this world that know the location of Old Hoy. Unless you're from around these parts you'll never hear about Old Hoy. And it's not on a map," Little George remarks.

"And there lies the ruse. The sheriff wants you and me alone with Lady to meet up with him and a hand full of his deputies at the old dirt road that leads into Old Hoy tomorrow night. Maybe with Lady in the hunt we can find out just what in the "Sand Hill'" is going on in Old Hoy. Before some old boy accidently walks up on these drug runners while he's deer hunting and gets shot."

CHAPTER 46

Old Hoy

A ruby red sun has gone down behind a bank of haze gray clouds. And a gentle southerly breeze rustles the light tanned colored prairie grass as everyone gets in place. As soon as Lady's paws hit the ground Little George notices a change in her body movement. "From the way Lady's is acting I believe she knows this place," Little George whispers.

"Yep--- I've been watching those ears standing straight up and her tail going ninety miles an hour. Then all of a sudden it stopped," Grandpa George says.

Sheriff Thomas gets out of his squid car and walks over to where Big George and Little George are standing and says, "What do you say we let Lady lose and follow her. She just might lead us right to the people we're looking for."

CHAPTER 47

Sheriff Thomas comes from a family of law officers. With a grandfather that was in law enforcement and two brother that still serve. Standing six foot four inches and a trim two hundred and fifty pounds most criminals know one look from his blue eyes and you might as well throw up your hands.

"Sounds like a plan to me. What do you think Little George?" Big George says.

Little George looks first at his Grandpa George then at Sheriff Thomas. "Might as well give it a try as big as this place is it will take us all night to check all the hiding places and we still might not find them."

Sheriff Thomas calls all his deputies on his radio to inform them of the plan. As Little George releases Lady. She makes a bee line for a spot where one dirt road joins another dirt road to make a Tee. From this point you can. Either turn right and head south. Or you can turn left and you'll be headed north through a large stand of hardwood trees left over from the big Logging Days.

Straining his eyes to see in the dark Grandpa George whispers, "I didn't see her turn Little George. Which way did she go?"

"She turned south. She's heading in the direction of the

two big ponds and that big clump of hardwood trees on the east side of the road."

As Grandpa George, Sheriff Thomas and Little George step off the road and into the ditch. They suddenly hear a dog barking in the distant. In an instance the booming sound of a rifle being fired echoes in the night. A short second later Little George hears a swirling sound past his head as a bullet pasts close by. "Everybody get down," Sheriff Thomas yells out.

After a few short minutes of quite. The men hear a truck engine cough a few times and start up. Now the sounds of grinding gears can be heard as someone shifts into other gears to gain a little speed.

After a short second the loud sound of banging from the truck can be heard echoing through the still night. As the trucks bottom hit's old washed out stump holes and the wheels roll over old rotted out fallen down trees, which are in its way.

After a short few minutes every ones nerves seems to have settle down a little except Lady's. When Little George finds Lady she's bearing her teeth and letting out a low growling sound from deep in her throat. As she stares at the dark entrance of a camouflaged tent nestled between two large Red Oak Trees.

As the deputies and Sheriff Thomas come running up to Ladies side to see what she is pointing at.

They all have their headlights on and their guns drawn. As they all stop in front of the partially hidden tent. Deputy Sheriff Mike Lowes reaches out and pulls back the tent flap and shines his flashlight inside. In an instance a high pitched voice from inside yells out, "Don't shoot!! Please Don't Shoot! --- I give up."

CHAPTER 48

After an hour of searching around the two ponds and a walk through the hard wood clumps Sheriff Thomas's radio comes to life with reports from his deputy sheriff's. The first to report in is Deputy Lee. As his voice crackles over the radio he reports, "We found a three quarter inch P.V.C. Pipeline about one hundred feet long running from one of the ponds to a gas operated pump hidden in a hollowed out log. And it runs out to a garden of some kind, "Over."

The next radio report comes in from Chief Deputy Hank Stubby. "Sheriff we got a full blown marijuana garden on the north side of this hard wood clump. And from what we can see in the dark it's a major garden operation we have here "Over."

After all of his deputies report in Sheriff Thomas and Little George go back to check on Lady.

Shining his headlight in Ladies direction Little George says, "There she is over by that big White Oak tree."

"What on earth is she chewing on Little George?" Sheriff Thomas ask as he shifts his light around to get a better view.

As Little George shines his head light on Lady he spies a rope, or cable in her mouth. "I'm not sure sheriff. But I think she's chewing on a rope, or maybe a cable."

"A rope--- let's have a look see," Sheriff Thomas says in an excited voice.

As they trained their head lights up into the tree top. They are amazed at what their eyes are seeing. Suspended up in the trees all wrapped up in big black cargo net's sets huge bundles of cut marijuana.

Just as Little George and Sheriff Thomas are getting over their big find. A voice comes over Sheriff Thomas's radio reporting a bunch more sightings of cargo nets suspended in other tree tops that other deputies have located.

"Folk's from what I've seen. I believe this is the drug smugglers the Texas law enforcement people and Louisiana law have been trying to catch. The only bad thing so far is. Somebody, or a bunch of drug runners got away in that truck that left out of here. So our job isn't finished. Not till I have all those crooks behind bars," Sheriff Thomas says.

"I think you hit the nail right on the head. What are you planning to do with that Jelly Head you caught?" Big George ask.

"Oh, I think we'll take him on in to jail and see if he wants to sing us a song. And tell us who the head honcho of this operation is?"

Looking at Sheriff Thomas with a frown on his face Little George mutters, "I just want to catch the person who shot Lady."

"Well that makes two of us. And By-Golly we'll get them," Grandpa George replies.

"Make it three of us," Sheriff Thomas says as he starts walking back to his car.

Driving up the driveway to Grandpa George's house Little George spies a thin pink streak in the east as the sun is getting ready to make its first appearance of the day. "Looks like a beautiful day in the making," Grandpa George mutters in a tired voice.

"I probably want see much of it. After I feed lady and myself I'm going to play dead in my bed," Little George says as he lets out a big yawn.

CHAPTER 49

Hide Out On Bundick Creek

"**M**an... that was a close call. We just got our butts out of Old Hoy just in time," Sam Long mutters.

"Yea... and driving like a bat-out-of-hell down these old gravel roads full of curves and sometimes on two wheels with no head lights on. I think I might have messed in my pants," Luke Holiday growls.

Taking a puff on his ready roll cigarette Sam said, "Well you had a choice. You could have stayed and got arrested by the sheriff like Goggle Eye did. That away you'd get three hot's and a cot and your pants would be clean."

Gazing at Sam seated on a stump on the other side of the camp fire Luke said with a snarl, "I know all about them three hot's and a cot Sam. But the thing that bothers me the most is how in the hell did the sheriff and his men find us. That's what I want to know?"

Thumping his cigarette into the camp fire and watching the hot embers swirl up into the dark night sky Sam says, "A couple of days back some old coot came stumbling around one late afternoon. Old Peewee let out a bark and I shot off a round up in the air to spook the old fella off. And he took off running like a "Spotted-ass-Ape"' through the woods and kept on going. Now he just might have reported that to the sheriff."

Carl Lopper is squatted down by the fire holding a tin cup full of coffee made out of parched corn. After taking a slow pull on his cup Carl lets the warm liquid slowly slide down his throat. After a short pause Carl says, "I think I know how the sheriff found us out."

"I'd dam well would like to know. We had a good thing going. Now it's all gone to hell in a hand bag. And we probably lost over half a million dollars in dope and equipment. Not to mention the fact they probably have Goggle Eye in jail by now," Sam says in shock.

"You know they have him Sam. And before the sun comes up tomorrow, old Goggle Eye will be singing like a Carney," Luke mutters.

Setting his tin cup down on the ground Carl stands up and stretches his six foot frame to its fullest. He knows the two men staring at him wouldn't hesitate to kill him if it comes down to saving their hides. Looking Sam in the eyes Carl said in a deep voice, "Remember, when you told me to take the Chesapeake Gyp down the road and kill her."

"Yea... I remember giving you that little chore Carl," Sam says as he swats at a mosquito buzzing around his head.

Rubbing a two week growth of beard Carl says, "Yea... well the only problem with that was you gave me a shot gun with one shell in it. When I got to the end of the road I threw her out the truck and into the ditch and shot her. But the one shot didn't do the job. She was still alive, when I hopped back in the truck."

"So what happened then?" Luke ask with venom dripping in his voice.

"I picked her up and took her to old man George's Veterinary Clinic before someone came driving around the curve and seen me. Old George and that crippled up grandson of his took the dog in. I figured from the looks of the dog it wouldn't live long,"

Throwing the little bit of coffee that's left in his tin cup into the fire Luke says, "We got to find out if that dog is still alive, because she can lead the cops right to us. And another thing to consider is the people around her. They just might become a big problem too. For one thing, that old man and his grandson can identify you Carl. After they have you it's just a matter of connecting the dots. And after that's done it's all downhill for everyone."

"That's enough talking for tonight. Let's get some sleep and in the morning I'll drive out to old man Mars Noah's shack and talk to his son Link. Maybe he can do a little creeping around and find out if that dog is still alive and if it is, who has her. Once we know that. Then we can make a plan to take care of her permanently," Sam says.

CHAPTER 50

Laying on his back in the dark in his sleeping bag listening to the noises of the forest, Carl keeps thinking. "How on earth did I get mixed up with this bunch of loser's?" After a short few minutes Carl rolls onto his side to get a better view of the time on his wrist watch from the light of the dying camp fire. The hands showed 3:00 a.m.

Rolling out of his sleeping bag Carl decides to walk down the bluff bank and out onto the snow white sand bar. Pulling out a blue pack of "Bugler Smoking Tobacco'" he pours a small amount of tobacco onto a white thin piece of paper.

Putting the pack of Bugler back into his shirt pocket he rolls the paper with the tobacco between his two thumbs and fingers a couple of times. Then he licks the paper with his tongue. Finding a match in his other shirt pocket Carl strikes the match on the zipper of his pants. Once the match flares to life he takes a long pull on his roll-your-own cigarette and exhales and watches the blue smoke drift over the dark water.

Squatting down on his heels and staring at the reflection of the stars on the water. Carl can hear a large fish slapping its tail on the top of the water trying to scare the smaller fish out into the deeper water where they'll become its next meal.

He knows how the smaller fish feel. He also knows in time

he has to get away from being a drug runner and away from this bunch before something bad happens to himself, or someone else. Thumping his cigarette into the water Carl heads back up the bluff bank and crawls into his sleeping bag.

CHAPTER 51

Hearing the dull thud of a piece of wood being thrown onto the fire causes Carl to open one eye. Sam is filling the coffee pot with creek water and placing the pot on a wire mesh screen over the hot coals. Gazing over the top of Sam's head Carl can see Luke standing on the sand bar with a towel and a bucket full of water using a bar of homemade soap taking a "G.I. Bath.'"

After a breakfast of burnt egg's and over fried French Fries all washed down with two tin cups of black coffee. Sam stands up and stretches out his six foot frame. He reaches into his shirt pocket and pulls out a twist of "Cotton-Bowl-Chewing Tobacco." Reaching into his pants pocket he unfolds a Case knife and processes to cut a plug off the twist and places it in the right side of his jaw.

Sam mumbles as he glances first at Luke than Carl, "We need to find that dog and the people who are taking care of her. If we don't the whole bunch of us will be sent up the river without a paddle."

"Let's break camp and head for Mars Noah's house on Ten Mile Creek. Old man Mars been running Moonshine for years and Link knows everybody for miles around here," Luke says.

"Yea...maybe we can hire Link to creep around and find

out where that dog is," Sam replies.

"I hope so. Otherwise we just might be staying at Angola Prison for a long time," Sam says looking at Carl.

CHAPTER 52

Sugar Town

January rolls around in a flash and Little George has his fingers crossed and hopes he's given all the love and attention Lady needs. He's watched her go from a three legged retriever to a hard working raccoon hunter. And he didn't do it all by himself. Judy has run as many steps in the woods as he has. Even when his stump would get raw from the rubbing Judy would take over for him.

As of right now Little George is driving Grandpa George's Red International Pickup Truck. And he's headed to his first Grand- Nite-Championship tryout in Sugar Town. As he glances over at Judy setting next to the passenger's door and Lady has the middle of the seat. He can tell the three of them have a bad case of the jitters coming on. As his mind wonders on the dos and don'ts of the tryout he suddenly hears Judy voice saying, "You better slow down Little George the WYE is right up ahead."

Making a right hand turn off Highway Twenty Six onto Highway One Hundred and Thirteen, Little George down shifts the truck into second gear. As he regains a little speed he push's in the clutch again and moves the shifter into third gear. It's a seven mile drive down a dark and winding road where the houses are a mile apart.

In a matter of a few minutes Little George spies a green sign with big white block lettering saying "SUGAR TOWN.'" A few feet further and they come to the heart of this small community with a four way stop sign.

For years Sugar Town's claim to fame was its world's smallest post office.

Putting the head lights on high beam Little George starts looking around for directions to get to where the tryout is being held.

All of a sudden there on the bottom of one of the stop signs someone has taped a cardboard sign with a big hand drawn black arrow pointing to the direction of the tryout.

Turning left and driving three hundred feet further Little George spots another cardboard sign tacked to the side of a pine tree saying "PARKING" written with big bold letters and a big black arrow pointing the way down a lane, which is lined with pine trees and an old rusted fence that's fallen down.

Judy spies a man with a flashing yellow light waving them through an old wooden gate that's seen its better days. And to their right sets a line of all makes and models of cars and trucks parked in a straight line.

"I guess this is our parking spot?" Little George says as he turns hard to the right and stomps on the brakes and stops.

Looking around in all directions Judy mutters, "Where on earth do you check in?"

"I'm not too sure, but from the looks of all those coal oil lanterns burning over by that big hay wagon. My guess is it might be a good place to start."

As they both approach the hay wagon with Lady in tow

Little George spots a makeshift desk made out of two wooden barrels and two, two-by-twelve wooden blanks laid on top the barrels. And to his surprise he recognizes the face of the big man seated behind the check in desk. "How are you Mr. Falter?"

The man glances up at Little George's face through the dim yellow glow of the coal oil lanterns. Little George can tell by the expression on Mr. Falter's face he's having a problem placing him. But when Little George hands him his entry form with his name on it Mr. Falters face brakes into a big smile. "Well I'll be Dad-Burn-It."' I've known two other George's in my time on this earth and now I'm looking at the third one standing right in front of me."

Standing up from his chair and grasping Little George's right hand with his big callous hand. Pumping it up and down until Little George thinks Mr. Falter is going to dislocate his right shoulder.

Mr. Falter turns his head sideways and spits a stream of tobacco juice from his month. If you look at Mr. Falter its plane to see this man is a product of his times. Because he's dressed in a pair of faded Liberty blue overalls and a scoffed up pair of brown brogans are on his feet. And it's not hard to tell what he does for a living. If you look real close you can tell his shirt is made from a one hundred pound printed sack of dairy feed. And perched on top his head sets a straw hat that's seen its better days.

Mr. Falter squints his dark beady eyes at Little George. "You know son, I can still remember playing basketball against your grandpa back when he played for Fairview and I played for Sugar Town. And till this day I still believe your grandpa has the sharpest elbows of anybody I've ever played against."

Once the laughter subsides Little George says, "I remember him talking about some of the games he played in and the places. I remember him naming places like Pitkin, Elizabeth, Oakdale, Kinder, Reeves, Oberlin, Forest Hill and Sugar Town."

"Yep…I've been in all those places myself. Well I guess I better get up on this here hay wagon and get this tryout on the road, or we'll be here all night."

Mr. Farley climbs up a small wooden ladder that's attached to the wagon bed. Once on top he waves his big arms high in the air to get the attention of the crowd. "Ok folks let me have your attention for a minute now. Before we can get this thing started I need all of the contestants to walk over here and draw their starting position number."

After Little George pulls his number, he walks back to where Judy and Lady are standing by Grandpa George's truck.

"What's our starting tag number?" Judy ask.

"I pulled number four… I sure hope it's a lucky one for us. Because I spied some tough competition while I waited to pull my number."

After a slow thirty minutes of waiting their number is finally called. As the group comes to the gate leading into the woods Little George spies a squat built man with a Lincoln style beard wearing a black and gold Fairview High School Panthers cap. The man introduced himself as Mr. Tom Lark from the Black Jack Community. And he'll be their Timer.

The two Counters are Nate Orr from Dry Creek and Pat Willow from the Six Mile Community. After the interdiction Mr. Lark reads the rules and asked if everyone is ready.

CHAPTER 53

O nce in the woods everybody turns on their headlights and makes the necessary adjustments to their clothing and head lights.

After checking his equipment Little George give Lady his "Go find the raccoon Lady" and she takes off with her nose to the ground.

After a ten minute run Lady is barking at the top of her lungs. On Lady's first call of Treed, Little George is four seconds late on calling her Treed.

On her second Treed he gets it right on the money and she holds her position till their counter and the two timers arrive.

Rubbing the back of his neck Mr. Lark gazes down at Lady setting by Little George's leg and says, "That's not bad for a dog on her first tryout son."

At the end of the competition Mr. Farley steps up onto the hay wagon. Using his best booming voice, which echoes through the woods. He starts his grand announcement of the winners. "Ok now folks a little quite please," Mr. Farley says in his best statesmanship voice.

After a few fake cough's he continues. "Now in fourth place we have Mr. Tom Hurley from Oberlin." After this announcement a little cheer goes up from the crowd.

"All right now folks calm down now," Mr. Farley says.

"And now we have in third place a young man out of the Flat Creek Community by the name of Little George."

Again a little cheer goes up and a few barks from the dogs can be heard. The loudest cheer comes from Judy in the back row and the loudest and longest barking comes from Lady.

"Ok---ok now people," Mr. Farley's voice echoes over the old watermelon field. "In second place out of the Black Jack community we have Mr. Mike Arthur." As soon as the name is said a big cheer is heard and a concerto of barking raddles the night air.

At the end of a three minute ovation Mr. Farley takes back command. "Here we go folks--- in first place out of Red Bluff we have Mr. Ty Odom." A few wolf whistles goes off and a Blue Tick hound starts howling in the back of the crowd.

After a short round of cheers and a few barks and howls from the dogs. Everyone quitted down for a few minutes. Then the hand shaking and slaps on the back commenced and the talk turned to the next tryout.

"I guess we better get on down the road. It's getting late," Little George says.

"Lady and I are ready when you are. I'm tuckered out and ready for a good hot bath."

On the drive home everyone in the cab is a little bit nervous about their big win tonight. Not paying attention to his driving Little George isn't aware of his zigzagging on the road.

"I wish you would stop that zigzagging Little George. You're about to make me sea sick and Lady almost fell off the seat," Judy says in an aggravated voice.

"I'm sorry. It's just that I'm all worked up over our big win tonight,"

"For me the best part came when Mr. Farley read out the names of the winners and your name was in third place," Judy giggles.

"Yea--- but did you see Mr. Hope. I believe he might have swallowed his chewing tobacco when my name was called out."

"Why do you say that?" Judy replies as she looks over at Little George.

"Because right after my name was called out he started gagging, coughing, and spitting. And when I turned around to see what all the fuss was about. He was bent over trying to catch his breath.

That's, when I ran over to see if I could help him. Then I noticed his face had turned blue.

That's, when his son Curly ran over and started pounding on his daddy's back. After a couple of hard smacks between his shoulder blades, I saw something fly out of Mr. Hope's mouth.

When he finally sucked in a couple of big gulps of air he turned to Curly and says. Dam son... you don't have to try and kill me."

CHAPTER 54

The next morning Little George slept right through Sammy's ritual and almost missed breakfast. He guesses it goes to show a person is not good at listening, but does a good job at smelling. As Little George sets down to a plate of French toast, and syrup, along with a large glass of coffee milk, he can feel his Grandpa George eyeballing him. So to keep him off balance Little George decides to give his Grandpa George the good news voluntary. "We had a good night last night. Lady placed third in her very first time out."

Taking a big pull of coffee from his big white navy mug Grandpa George says, "Third place. Why I would've never guessed she would do that good."

Shaking his head up and down Little George replies, "We got off to a slow start at first then Lady put her noise to the ground and the race was on. She worked her heart out and never stopped till she had a raccoon up a tree. Mr. Lark thinks Lady did great on her first time out."

"And how is your assistant doing?" Grandma Gracie ask with a grin on her face.

Not knowing the true meaning behind the question Little George decides to play it safe. "Great... Judies right there in the middle of everything. And she keeps the time records and helps me keep Lady ready to go."

Little George can see a sparkle in Grandma Gracie's eyes as he said these words. And a small grin shows on Grandpa George's face as he nods his head towards Grandma Gracie.

"Ok now. While you two get ready for church and I'll head for the barn and do a little feeding," Grandpa George says as he gets up from the table and heads through the doorway.

CHAPTER 55

Ten Mile Creek

Bouncing over a wooden creosote bridge which spans Ten Mile Creek, Luke growls, "Dam… Sam you better slow down. One of these days you're going to end up in that darn creek."

"What's eaten you Luke? The devils got you by the toes," Sam chuckles softly.

Giving Sam a look that could kill Luke says, "Don't you worry about the devil Sam. You better worry about me."

Carl is seated by the passenger's side door with his hand on the door handle ready to jump out if Sam and Luke decide to shot it out.

"Slow down Sam. Around the next curve you'll see a dirt road on the right hand side. That's the Old Ox-Slew Road. And down at the dead end sets a small clap-board shanty that Link Noah and his daddy Mars live in," Luke says.

After a twenty minute drive through ruts some as deep as the truck and around fallen trees. They finally reach a small clearing. "Dam… how in the hell did Mars find this place?" Sam ask.

"Only the good lord knows," Carl replies as he looks around.

According to the good folks living on Six Mile Creek the Ox-Slew was formed many years ago. It was a shallow place on the creek bank where the Lumber Jacks would skid the logs down into the creek with the help of Oxen. Once the logs, were floated. Men would ride the logs downstream to a big saw mill.

"Look… there's Mars shack park behind that big White Oak tree," Sam says pointing his finger.

After the three men get out of the truck Luke ask, "Where in the hell do you think that old Coot is?"

Suddenly a gravelly sounding voice behind the three men spoke up and says, "Right behind you three "Knuckle Heads"' and looking at you through the sights of this here twelve gage shot gun."

"Hold up Mars… don't shoot! We come to see you for a little business deal," Sam's voice crackled.

"What kind of business deal?"

CHAPTER 56

Mars Noah has the body built of a wooden fifty-five gallon barrel. And his face is covered with a dark brown beard streaked with gray. Perched beneath a wooly set of eye brows are two small dark beady eyes, which are always moving around like a radar forever taking in the scenery. Most of the folks around Six Mile Creek who know Mars say he has the disposition of a Jackass. But the rumor around here is Old Mars has done some time in Angola State Prison for killing a man. And now he's out and he has a big chip on his shoulder.

"If you'll lower that scatter gun Mars we just might be able to work out a little deal that could help us all out," Luke mumbles.

Gazing at his three uninvited guests Mars takes his time lowering his shot gun. "Ok boys it's your dime. Let's hear what you got to say."

The outside temperature has already climbed into the mid fifty's, yet Sam pulls a handkerchief from the back pocket of his faded jeans. He proceeds to wipe the sweat that's popped out on his forehead as he said in a hurried voice, "We came looking for your son Link." All the while Sam is keeping an eye on the shot gun in Mars hands.

"Link's not here. He's busy down by the creek watching

my investment," Mars replies.

Sam, Luke and Carl look at each other with a puzzled look on their faces. They're thinking maybe the tails they've heard about Old Mars is all wrong.

Shrugging his shoulders and gazing at Mars holding the twelve gage shot gun with his two fingers on both triggers Luke snorts, "We got a little problem. And we thought Link could do a little creeping around and gather some information for us Mr. Mars."

Dressing the three men down with his small dark eyes Mars ask, "Just exactly what is your problem Mr.?"

Looking down at his dust covered boots Luke replies, "We had a little drug operation going on in Old Hoy for a few years then the sheriff and his boys busted it up a few nights back. But our biggest problem is a dog and the people who saved her life."

Looking Luke up and down while spitting a stream of dark brown tobacco juice out from between his fingers and wiping his hand on his bib overalls Mars says with a small grin on his face, "Yep... I can see where a dog just might cause you three boys a big problem."

"Do you think Link can help us out?" Luke ask.

Rubbing the back of his stubby neck and gazing at the three men Mars replies, "I'm not sure. You'd have to ask him yourself."

Giving Mars his "What in the Hell Look" Sam replies, "Where can we find him?"

Pointing his shot gun in the direction of an old rusted yellow Bulldozer with the front blade missing Mars says, "You feller's hop up on that old D-7 and I'll take you down to where

Link's at."

CHAPTER 57

After a thirty minute ride through briar patches as big as houses and ruts as deep as a two story building and tree limbs slapping them in the face and tearing at their clothes. Sam, Luke, and Carl are holding on for dear life. Merciful the Bulldozer finally pulls up to a clearing and stops.

"All right all you hanger on. You can get off now," Mars growls.

Jumping off the Bulldozer and down onto the ground the three men start flicking leaves and mud off their shirts and pants. Sam lost his green John Deere hat, when the Bulldozer passed under a low hanging limb. In the back of his mind Sam has a hunch Mars did it on purpose.

Wiping his face Sam growls, "Dam I almost fell off this thing three times."

"Now don't get your draws in a wad boys. It's just a little further. Just follow me," Mars says with a gleam in his eyes.

After a ten minute walk through the woods they come to a small clearing. Looking up the first thing a person's eyes sees is a large camouflage netting covering the entire area. On the opposite side of the clearing sets a large copper still with a column of smoke swirling up into the air. To the right of the still sets a Black Jack Tree. And under it sets a lean-to filled with different size wooden barrels and a large stack of white propane steel tanks.

Waving his arms in an arch Mars says proudly, "Well boys... welcome to my investment."

All three men are stunned at what they're seeing. They just stand glued to the ground with their mouths wide opened. Because standing right before their eyes is the largest "Moonshine Still"' anyone has every laid eyes on.

"Wow," Sam utters. "You've got one hell of an operation going on here Mars."

"I like to think I do," Mars dead pans as he holds his shot gun in both his hands.

"Where's Link? He's the man we came out here to talk to," Sam said slowly as he swats at a pesky mosquito buzzing around his head.

"Why he's right behind you with an A.K.47 aimed right at you boys," Mars replies with a soft chuckle.

Hearing these words come out of Mars mouth causes all three men to slowly turn around to get a peek at Link. But to their surprise no one's in sight.

With his patients wearing thin Sam growls, "Hell Mars... what kind of bullshit is this. We come all this way out here to talk to Link. And all we get is a bull dozer ride from hell and games."

Mars little beady eyes narrowed as he heard Sam saying these words. Cupping his hands around his mouth Mars yells out, "Link... let off a few rounds at these here bad ass boys. But don't hit none of them."

In a matter of three short seconds twenty rounds of bullets pepper the ground around the three men's feet. Dirt flies up into their eyes and leaves swirl up into the air around the three men.

After a moment of coughing and rubbing the dirt out of their eyes Sam shouts out, "Shit... you must be nuts Mars."

"Maybe so Sam, but not nuts enough to trust you three Knot Heads," Mars says with a big grin on his face. "Why I wouldn't trust you all as far as I could pick you up and throw you."

Out of the corner of his eye Carl spies a limb on a tree moving. "Why I'll be dam... that limb on that White Oak tree just moved. And if my eyes aren't fooling me, I believe it's a gun barrel."

"Now... you boys are getting the hang of it. And now all you have to figure out is how many of them limbs are real," Mars replies with a smirk on his bearded face.

"We didn't come here for trouble Mars. We really came here to talk to Link about doing a little creeping for us," Sam says.

"Creeping around for what?" A deep voice said from behind the three men.

Turning in the direction the voice came from. The men are surprised to see a six foot bush holding an A.K.47.

After getting out of his brush camouflage Link walks over and stands by his father's side. "Not by any chance you fella's are the same bunch that got run out of Old Hoy?" Link says with sarcasm dripping in his voice.

Looking at each other Sam said drily, "That's why we came out here. We need someone who can do a little snooping around while not drawing attention to himself."

"Let me ask a few questions. First is. How much money

are you talking about? And next is. Just what is this job all about?" Mars ask.

Luke flips a piece of dried mud off his shirt sleeve with his finger. Then he turns his gaze at Mars with the twelve gage shot gun still in his hands. Mars is standing not ten feet in front of Sam, Carl, and himself. Shifting his eyes to his left and there stands Link with that A.K-47 and his finger is still on the trigger.

"The answer to your first question is one thousand dollars for two weeks work. And the answer to your second question is. Find out where this Chesapeake Bay retriever is. And, who has her. That should be easy enough for you to do Link," Luke mutters.

"Yea...Umm-humm...sounds pretty easy, but the moneys all wrong," Link replies.

"What in the hell do you mean the moneys all wrong?" Sam asked harshly.

Link easily moved the barrel of his A.K.-47 slightly more in line with the three men standing in front of him. Seeing this move causes a great concern for the three drug runners. "Well the way I got figured out. If I work two weeks for you three men I should get paid two thousand instead of one thousand. What do you think Pa?" Link says looking at his father.

Mars replies, "Why that sounds mighty reasonable to me. How about it boys?"

"OK... it's a deal. One of us will check in every other day with you Link," Sam said. All the while he's digging in his front pocket. After a short struggle Sam pulls out a wad of money and hands the money to Link and says, "Here's your first payment."

After Mars and Link count the money, Mars turns around and says, "Why don't you boys mount up. And I'll ride you out of here and back to your truck."

CHAPTER 58

On the ride back out Mars takes it a little slower. After all these men are like money in the bank. Maybe if this deal works out a long term relationship could develop.

Ten minutes into the ride Sam's curiosity finally got the best of him. Scratching a four day old beard Sam gives Mars a sideways glance and ask, "Mars... mind if I ask you a question?"

Mars looks hard at Sam. "Go ahead Sam ask your question."

"I've been thinking. Ever since we got here it seems to me that you've known we were coming. Why even our little ride through the woods and reaching the clearing only to find Link hidden in a tree. So the way I got it figured out somebody's been spying on us."

Mars lets out a chuckle and pulls back on the hand brake stopping the Bulldozer. "You got it all wrong Mr. Sam-know-it-all. The way I knowed you were coming is. I heard you coming."

After hearing this the three men had a dazed and confused look on their faces. "How in the world can you hear us coming Mars?" Carl ask.

"Very simple when you know how to do it. Back, when I was in Vietnam my job was to operate a listening post. The Army dropped thousands of listening devices called "Geophones."' With these Geophones we could hear a man walking in the jungles. And it would tell us which way he's headed and how many men are walking. That's how we kept up with them "Victor Charlie's.'"

"So you have some of those things around here?" Sam ask.

"Umm-hmm…A couple of years back Uncle Sam had a yard sale and I bought two dozen of these Geophone and placed them out where they would do the most good in protecting my investment."

"Maybe we should have used something like that instead of a dog," Sam says.

After a short ride Mars's place comes into view. "Ok boys this is your bus stop," Mars says as he pulls back on the hand break of the Bulldozer.

After the men jump off the Bulldozer Sam gazes in Mars direction. "We'll be in touch."

As Mars grabs the door knob of his shanty he turns around. "Yea…I bet you will."

CHAPTER 59

Mittie

Between school work and what little time they have for training this week flew by in a hurry. The distant from Flat Creek to Mittie is about three miles as the crow flies. As you head east on Highway-Twenty-Six you better keep both eyes wide open, or you'll miss the two houses and the lone grocery store that makeup Mittie.

Tonight there's a nip in the air and it feels like its blowing off a huge block of ice. The only problem with this kind of temperature is. If you don't have enough clothing on you'll feel the freezing cold close to your body and your nose will start dripping. Then on the other hand if you put too much clothing on and you run through the woods for thirty minutes. The next thing you know you're soaking wet with sweat under all the clothing you have on. Then after a short break and while you're standing still you'll start freezing to death. So no matter how you dress it's probability going to be wrong.

"From the looks of all the tail lights in that old corn field they must want us to park in there," Judy says pointing her finger.

After Little George parks Grandpa George's truck. Judy, Lady and Little George decide to do a little exploring.

After a short walk Little George spots a familiar sight. The same hay wagon and makeshift desk is the same one used in Sugar Town. Even Mr. Farley is here. And the timers and counters are all mingling around shaking hands and talking loud.

All of a sudden out of the corner of his eye Little George spies a familiarly looking old rusted beat up white Chevy pickup truck with the driver side rear finder missing.

"Hold up a minute Judy, I think I see something familiar?" Little George says in an anxious voice.

"What is it?"

"I believe I spotted that beat up white truck the stranger was driving the day he brought Lady to the clinic all shot up."

"Where... all I see are pickup trucks. There must be at less twenty, or more parked in here Little George."

Pointing his finger in the direction of a huge Evangeline Oak tree Little George says, "Right over there--- that beat up white truck with the driver's side rear finder missing. That's got to be the truck. There can't be that many trucks around these parts that look like that."

"Ok...but how on earth can you prove that's the truck?"

Looking down at Lady with her big dark brown eyes shining in the dark Little George says, "We have someone with us who knows if that's the truck. After all she rode in it."

As they take their time walking a little closer towards the truck Little George hears a deep growing noise coming from

Lady's mouth and her teeth are showing in the dark. "I believe that's enough proof for me. Lady knows this truck," Little George whispers.

Looking around Little George decides to walk a little closer to get a better look at the license plate hanging on the rear bumper of the truck by a strand of bailing wire. All of a sudden Little George hears muffled voices coming from inside the cab of the truck.

Stopping in his tracks Little George whispers to Judy, "Let's ease back a little there's two people sitting inside."

Walking back to where the coal oil lanterns are giving off a little light Little George says, "We need to stick close together. I don't know why that man is here, or who the other person in the cab with him is. But you can bet your last dollar bill they're not talking about raccoon hunting."

After signing in and pulling his starting position number Little George walks back to where Judy and Lady are setting on the truck tailgate. After glancing around Little George sets down by Judy.

"I need to ask you something Little George," Judy says.

Little George gazes at Judy by using his head light and replies in a suspicious voice, "Go ahead and ask me Judy."

Looking down at her hands and kicking her legs out Judy says, "Well... for whatever the reason is it. That when you put a bunch of men and dogs together. It's not long the talk turns to great dog's and their hunting feats and what a man has done in his hunting exploits. And after a little while it's a big round of belly laughs. And the dogs start barking and howling none stop."

Adjusting his head light so Judy can't see his face Little George remarks, "I guess it's a man thing."

Before this conversion can go any further Little George hears Mr. Farley calling out number one. "That's our number. We better get a move on and get up there."

CHAPTER 60

Standing by a brand new shiny aluminum gate, which leads into the woods are their new time keeper Mr. Joey Le-Blanc. And their two counters Mr. Abe Spencer, and Mr. Sam Moss.

After all the interdiction are made. And the rules read they all head into the woods together.

As soon as Little George says, "Go find the raccoon."

Lady takes off on a run and Little George and Judy have a hard time keeping up with her. In a matter of ten minutes Lady stops and taps a tree and looks up and barks four times.

As Little George runs up to her. He yells out at the top of his lungs, "I got a tree here."

After everyone shows up huffing and puffing Mr. Le-Blanc and the two counters verify there is indeed a raccoon up in the tree. The time is recorded and the counters make their mark as one treed.

"Ok folks shall we try one more?" Mr. LeBlanc says as small puffs of warm air escape from his mouth and swirl up into the cold night air in the form of white smoke.

Back on the run again Lady makes a run through a slew

and down the sandy banks of Whisky Chitto Creek. After a short minute she turns and heads for a Pin Oak tree covered in Muscadine Grape vines.

With her noise to the ground she makes one round of the tree then taps the tree with her front paw and raises her head and opens her mouth and lets out one long continues howl.

Running as fast as he can to the spot where Lady is at Little George begins shining his head light up into the branches of the tree. In a few short minutes he spies three sets of bright eyes blinking and yells out, "I got three raccoons over here in this tree."

As soon as everybody shows up and makes their mark on the Tally Paper. It's agreed it's time for a short break to catch their breaths.

Mr. LeBlanc and the two counters hold a short meeting amongst themselves. After their meeting is over its decided Lady will be way ahead of the other dogs and they'll call Lady's run completed.

Walking back to the truck Little George keeps thinking about the white pickup truck parked under the big tree with two people inside. "I still wonder about, who the two people are in that truck?"

"I don't have a clue Little George, but I bet Lady does. The only problem with letting her go around that bunch of people is one of them has already shot her. And if they can do that to a dog imagine what they will do to you and me,"

"Your right, it's best to let the sheriff handle them."

Shifting his head light around Little George says, "Not to change the subject but I'm hungry as a Grizzly Bear coming out of hibernation. Let's head to the truck and check on our sandwiches. And while we eat I can feed and water Lady."

As they're walking back to Grandpa George's truck Little George notices the banged up white truck is no longer under the tree. Walking a little further he thinks he's caught a glance of a shadow darting behind the trucks parked in front of his grandpa's truck. "Did you see what I seen, or am I getting a little daffy with all this Old Hoy drug stuff and Lady getting shot."

"I thought I seen something out of the corner of my eye too. And the way Lady is acting it's not a raccoon," Judy whispers back.

Walking slowly and shinning their lights around Little George and Judy finally reach the truck.

Opening the driver's side door Little George pulls out an old broken wooden hoe handle he sawed off to make into a long night stick.

Anticipating trouble he put it behind the seat just in case somebody wants to give them a hard time.

There's nothing like "Dough Popping'" someone upside the head with a piece of wood to get their attention.

Judy reaches in and grabs the brown paper bag off the passenger's side floor board that has their sandwiches and drinks. While Little George gets Lady's dog food and water bowl out from behind the seat along with his homemade night stick. Everyone settles down and starts enjoying their food.

After Little George takes a few bits of his "Hog Head Cheese'" sandwich he gazes down at Lady and notices she's quit eating her food and is looking at a green pickup truck with a man sitting inside it wearing a white baseball cap on his head.

"Don't move, or look to your left. I think we may have a visitor?"

After a minute passes a skinny man with long hair and a stringy goatee with a menacing grin gets out of the truck and walks up to Judy and Little George and says, "Well--- well if it isn't Mr. and Miss Goody Two Shoes."

Giving the man his best stair Little George replies in a brusquely voice, "And who do my eyes spy. None other than Link Noah,"

"Yea--- the last person on earth you would want to see while you are eating," Judy says with a voice dripping with sarcasm.

Looking down in the direction of the low snarling and growling noise Little George can see Lady's pearly white teeth showing from under her raised lips. He knows if he doesn't do something in the next few seconds Ladies going to get a bit of human flesh along with her dog food.

"Link why don't you get out of here before you get ate up by a dog, or better yet, before somebody calls the law,"

"Alright Little George you and your three legged dog wins this round. There will be another time and another place," Link replies smugly as he backs up and walks away into the night.

"That's one knot head that gives me the creeps," Judy says.

"I agree with you Judy. That whole family is a little creepy if you ask me."

Off in the distance they can hear the echoing sounds of dogs barking and men hollering at the top of their lungs. Every once in a while a cow horn is sounding off. With all that's going on with Link. Little George almost forgot why they're here.

"Come on Judy. Let's go and see how the tryout are coming alone. That way we can forget about that Jelly Head Link Noah."

CHAPTER 61

After two hours of run time. The tryout finally come to an end. And Mr. Farley makes his accession onto the top of the hay wagon bed and starts his announcement of this night's winners. In his usual grand tone of voice he begins naming the place finishers. "Ok now folks let's have a little quite now. We have in fourth place Mr. Slim Hanks out of the Six Mile Community."

After a short "Ada- Boy Slim" from the crowd Mr. Farley moves on to the third place finisher. "Ok here we go now folks. We have in third place Mr. Lee Planks out of the Red Bluff Community." This time Little George hears a few barks from a couple of Blue Tick Hounds.

After a few cough's Mr. Farley announces the second place finisher. "And in a close second place finish we have Mr. Mike Arthur out of the Black Jack Community." This time a few, "that away to go Big Mike." can be heard and four, or five truck horns started honking. And the sounds can be heard echoing through the woods.

Gazing at Little George with a worried look on her face Judy says in a quizzically voice, "I hope they haven't forgotten about us."

"I hope so to. Lady did a great job on this run. Maybe we got first place this time?"

Raising his arm to gain the attention of the crowd Mr. Farley says, "Ok now folks here we go. We have in first place out of the Flat Creek Community a Mr. Little George and his Chesapeake Bay retriever named Lady."

After the announcement Little George is on cloud nine. The slaps on the back are coming fast and furies. Even Judy is catching a few slaps on her shoulders and Lady is getting her share of pats on the head and a few. "Atta a girl, way to go," are all so being heard.

As soon as the congratulations subside Little George grabs Judy by her arm. "Let's get out of here while we can."

All the way to Judy's house Little George keeps a wary eye out in the rear view mirror.

When he gets these feeling that something is not quite right with a person, or a situation. He sometimes has a cold chill run up his spine. He can tell by the way Lady is acting she senses Judy and he are uneasy about something.

"Crossing "Carpenters Bridge"" Little George lets out a sigh of relief and Judy says, "I never thought home could look so beautiful."

As Judy steps out of the truck the front porch light comes on. Someone has stayed up till Judy got home. "See you Monday at school," Little George says.

All the way home Little George keeps thinking about how Link acted so sure of himself. It kind of makes him think maybe Link doesn't know he's recognized the truck that brought Lady to his Grandpa George's clinic that faithful day.

Little George glances at Lady seated by the passenger's side door with her pink tongue hanging out. It's hard to believe she's suffered so much, yet she give's so much love and loyalty back.

CHAPTER 62

Sunday morning Sammy catches Little George in a deep sleep, but he did hear a familiar voice at his bedroom door saying a familiar phrase, "Revile, Revile up all hands." He hears his Grandpa George laughing as he walks away from the bed room door.

After a big gulp of coffee milk Little George looks at Grandpa George seated in his usual spot at the head of the table. Not able to hold back the good news of his first place win last night Little George says, "Bet you'll never guess where we placed last night?"

Looking at his big white navy mug and shaking his head sideways Grandpa George replies, "Probably no better than third place the way I got it figured."

"How about first place for starters," Little George crows with a big grin on his face.

Hearing the exchange of words between Big George and Little George, Grandma Gracie lets out a chuckle, "Well Mr. knows it all. What did I tell you?"

CHAPTER 63

After church on the ride home no one said a word. The weather for January is cool and clear, but with the sun out it makes the inside of the truck feels hot and stuffy

Bouncing over the cattle guard and coming to a stop on the side of the house Little George gets out of the truck and heads for his bedroom.

After a quick change into his everyday clothes he heads for Lady's pen. "Where are you and Lady headed for now?" Grandpa George ask.

"I thought a little down time would be great for Lady. So I'm thinking a little walk in the woods might do the trick."

"Alright, but don't be late for supper, or you'll never hear the end of it. Believe me when your grandma closes the kitchen. It want open up again till tomorrow morning."

CHAPTER 64

Walking out the back of the old barn and heading down the hill towards the woods Little George spies a young Sassafras tree growing at the edge of the forest.

A little further down an old cow trail Lady and Little George startle a young Cottontail Rabbit chewing on new clover leaves.

After a three hundred yard walk further Little George and Lady come to an old rotten broken down wooden gate, which leads into the woods.

Stepping over what little remains of the gate Little George and Lady enter the woods and follow an old forgotten wagon trail. That takes you through a canopy of Red Oak trees mixed in with White Oak, Pine, and Hickory trees.

A little further down the trail they reach a spot on Flat Creek everyone call's, "The Old Bridge."' But now only a few rotted wooden pilings are left to indicate there ever was anything here. Time and weather has erased the old bridge and little remains of the trail.

When the water level is low in the creek it's just a matter of taking off your shoes and rolling up your britches legs up to your knees.

Or you can cross an old tree trunk that fell across the creek many years ago. Little George turns around looking for Lady. "Come on girl you can make it."

Once across the creek he sets down and puts his shoes back on. Standing back up, Little George waits for Lady to complete her inspection of the creek.

After a one hundred yard walk they're standing at the edge of a forty acre field encircled by trees.

And if Little George and Lady are real quiet they might hear a Quail whistling his "Bob White'" call, or a lonely Brown Owl setting up in a tree hooting somewhere in the deep woods.

After a short walk north of the field Little George has found what he's looking for. It's a giant Hickory tree standing tall and majestic with its lower branches touching the ground as if it's trying to hide something.

Little George calls out to Lady, "Here girl, I found it."

This is the tree where the initials of his Great Grandparents all the way down to his father and mother are carved into the side of the tree.

Standing next to this grayish brown giant tree with its leaves gone from its branch's for the winter. And just knowing he's standing in the same spot as his ancestors once did makes a cold chill run up his spin and gives him Goose Bumps.

Spreading the small limbs apart, so he can walk up to the tree trunk. Little George can see some of the names and dates are still legible.

The early names carved into the tree are not as easy to see. Little George still wonders if he'll ever see his name alone side the names of his ancestors.

Looking up at the top is Mr. and Mrs. Cyprien 1845.

And next is Mr. and Mrs. Arstile.

And then his Grandpa George and Grandma Gracie dated 1946.

And right below their name is his father and mother with a date of 1970.

Finding a clean spot to set down Little George can't help but watch the way Lady keeps looking around the tree. She'll put her nose to the ground and sniff around for a bit. And come back to Little George and set down at his feet and look him in the eye.

Reaching out and petting her on the top of her head. "Looking for something girl?" Turning her head sideways and giving Little George a strange look. Lady lays back down at his feet.

Little George can hear something rustling the dry winter leaves on the forest floor.

Even now setting this still he can hear his heart beating and the blood rushing through his vines.

After a short time passes Little George hears a car turning off Highway Twenty Six onto The Cherry Grove's gravel road.

If he moves around just a little to get in a comfortable position Lady looks up at him with a look of concern in her big brown eyes.

After a time he feels the old feelings start to swirl around inside his head. So he decides to take an inventory of his life as it is so far.

CHAPTER 65

Little George begins with the loss of his mother, father, and sister. And the trauma of finding out he's lost half a leg.

And all the hell he raised while he was in the hospital trying to learn how to walk on a prosthetic leg.

Then the problems with trying to start all over at a new home with his grandparents and living with the memories of the ones he loved the most.

Then in the neck of time along comes a Chesapeake Retriever who's in worst shape then him. And she gives him unconditional love and understanding.

And now this first time feeling of being close to a beautiful girl, who thinks he can do anything.

He remember hearing his daddy saying to himself, when he was not sure of the outcome of a decision he has to make would be. "What-to-do-what-to-do."

Looking around at the woods, he notices the shadows of the trees are getting longer. Looking into Lady's big brown eyes

Little George says softly, "We better hightail it out of here Lady, or there want be any supper for us tonight."

Following Lady out of the woods the thoughts of the good times he and Joy sheared plays over in his mind. Like the times they played Horse with his Basketball. And the times spent eating the candy they bought at the five and dime store.

Wiping a tear from his eyes with his shirt sleeve Little George looks up at the setting sun and wonders if there really is a heaven.

Taking his time walking along the old cow trail Little George watches Lady circle a small Pine tree a couple of times then stops and sets down.

Walking over to the spot where Ladies looking at the ground Little George spots a shiny object sticking out of the sand.

Reaching down and picking the object up he recognizes the object as a plastic gold colored ring Joy lost a few years back while they were foot racing.

Wiping the sand off Little George places the ring in his pocket. Thinking maybe Joy is watching over him. Turning around and looking at Lady. "Come on girl we need to head home."

CHAPTER 66

"What the hells the matter with you Sam. somebody pissed in your cereal this morning?" Luke demands loudly.

Gazing at Luke and grinning Sam says, "I took a little ride last night out to Mittie were they're holding them Grand-Nite-Championship tryout's. Guess who I ran up on?"

"Hell how should I know? Maybe your X- Old Lady," Luke snorts.

Flicking the ashes off his cigarette Sam replies, "Better than that Luke. I saw that dog and them two kids. They got that Gyp entered in that Championship."

"Dam! That's good news,"

"You better know it. I also ran into Link and he's keeping an eye on them just like he said he would."

"Great... when can we take care of business?" Luke ask.

"Link gave me the dates and where they're having those tryouts. From the looks of things, I figure Grant will be our best place to hit them.

There should be a lot of people around for the final championship. And nobody will notice us moving around," Sam says with an evil smile.

All of this time Carl keeps looking at the camp fire listening to his cohorts plotting to kill two innocent kids and a dog that hasn't done nothing to them.

After a few minutes of listening Carl is wishing he's dead. Then he starts thinking how in the world can he warn the people they're in danger without Sam and Luke becoming suspicious of him. And having both of them turn on him and kill him?"

CHAPTER 67

Soap Stone

Little George can remember hearing the old folks standing around his Grandpa George's clinic talking and saying, "Yep--- when you get old time sure does fly." Well at seventeen years old a week flies by in a hurry. "How much further to Soap Stone Little George?" Judy ask.

"We just went through Grant. So about another five miles and we should be there. Why are you asking?"

"Well… ever since we turned off Highway Twenty Six, I've been watching a set of head lights following behind us."

Shaking his head and looking out the side view mirror Little George says, "That's about all we need is trouble way out here in these piney woods, where the houses are a country mile apart and not a light insight."

CHAPTER 68

When you hear someone say, "Its pitch black outside" they are not exaggerating. Without a full moon, or bright star light the miles of woods can get real dark. But when the clouds are low enough you can tell the locations of the cities just by the reflection off the clouds from the city lights.

After a short few minutes the truck headlights show a curve in the road. This causes Little George to slow down and shift into second gear.

After a mile, or two he spies a red light waving them to turn right. Taking it kind of easy they bounce over a wooden cattle guard and down a rutted red clay dirt road.

After a short drive through a hay field that's already been harvested Little George spots a line of pickup trucks backed up against a barbed wired fence. Little George looks at Judy and Lady and said, "This must be the place."

After stepping out the truck Little George does a quick look around trying to spot the beat up white pickup with the missing rear finder. "What are you looking for?" Judy ask.

"I guess I get the jumps ever since our little run in with Lark Noah and the things that happened at Old Hoy with the drug runners.

I just have a funny feeling somebody's always keeping an eye on us."

"Well if that's the case I got something in my back pocket that will really get Mr. Lark's attention if he comes snooping around wanting to start trouble,"

With a surprise look on his face Little George ask, "What on earth do you have Judy. I hope it's not a gun?"

"It's not that bad Little George. My older brother Mike gave it to me. He said all you have to do is pull it out of your back pocket and wrap it around a trouble makers head. And your troubles are over, but the trouble maker's problems are just beginning."

When Judy pulls out a chain Little George can hardly believe his eyes. "What is it?"

"It's an old Harley Davison motor cycle chain with one end taped up to act like a handle for you to hold on to it when you swing it around."

With his eyes wide open in amusement Little George says, "Between your motor cycle chain and my hickory black jack. I guess we should be safe." After saying this he hears Lady give a soft growl. "Oh and I forgot. We have Lady on our side too."

As they walk over to the hay wagon to sign in and pull their starting number Little George can't help but notice a new blue pickup truck setting off by itself in the far corner of the field.

He can tell the truck doesn't belong back here in the

woods. The four tires are way too big for the truck and the chrome rimes are a dead giveaway. And the way the truck sets on the ground he can tell there's something other than a regular truck engine under the hood.

"What are you staring at?" Judy ask as her gaze follows Little George's.

"That blue truck parked over there." Little George nods his head in the direction of the truck.

"What's so strange about that truck?"

"Well, the one thing that bothers me is why would a person put an outside lock and hasp on a new truck? And how many fancy trucks have you seen in these woods?"

Gazing a little longer at the truck Judy says, "I didn't see that. The only thing I can come up with is the person, who owns it doesn't want anybody digging in it when he's not around."

"Or maybe there's something valuable inside the truck only a person with the right key can open the door and get to it," Little George replies.

Gazing at Judy in the dim lighting and rubbing the back of his neck Little George says, "Let's go set on the truck tail gate for a while. All this detective work is giving me a headache. Before too long I'll be seeing a crook behind every tree in the woods."

After eating their hickory smoked ham sandwiches and drinking their Root Beer drinks and Lady finishes her dog food.

Little George picks up her bowl and places it behind the truck seat.

Looking around for a familiar face to walk with him to the hay wagon and finding none Little George says, "I better hop on over to the hay wagon and sign in and pull our starting number, or we want be in this tryout."

About twenty yards into his walk in the direction of the hay wagon, Little George notices a man leaning on an old beat up rusted black pickup truck with part of the windshield missing.

Taking in this scene a person might think this is a causal thing, a country man lounging around and taking in the action of the tryout. After a few more steps Little George starts thinking. "You're starting to see spooks and things, which make no since."

"Good evening Mr. Farley," Little George says, as he walked up to the hay wagon

Mr. Farley looks up from the newspaper he has in his hand. Little George can see a deep furrow on his brow as if he's in a deep concentration. "Well hello there Little George. Where is Judy and Lady tonight?"

Pointing his finger Little George replies, "Their setting on the tail gate of grandpa's truck. So I came over to register and pull my starting number for the tryout."

Gazing up at Little George through the dim coal oil lantern light Mr. Farley says, "I've counted up your points. And so far it seems you're in first place right now. So keep up the good work. And you just might take first place this year."

"Thank you Mr. Farley. I'll tell Judy the good news."

After Little George pulls his starting number he puts it in his pants pocket. Turning around he starts walking slowly back towards his Grandpa George's truck. On his walk back Little George looks for the man, who he just seen on his way to the hay wagon earlier. But not a soul is in sight.

Walking slowly to where Judy and Lady are. Little George hears Judy say, "Welcome back lone lost red headed kid. What's our starting position tonight?"

"I didn't take time to look at the number,"

Holding it up high so he can see the number with his head light Little George says, "We got number three tonight."

After spending an hour setting on the truck tailgate and turning their heads around at the sights and sounds of men hollering and dogs howling and cow horns blowing into the night air.

Little George finely hears their number being called out. "Here we go. I hope we have a good run tonight and we don't run into anything in the woods other than raccoons."

"Well… if there's something other than raccoons hiding out in the woods. I got just the thing for them," Judy mumbles as she pats the back pocket of her faded jeans.

CHAPTER 69

After the introduction are made and the rules are read everybody starts walking into the woods. The wind tonight seems to come from several different directions at one time. And this is the last thing Little George needs for Lady. With a cold wind bouncing off the trees at different times it creates a swirling affect. And when a dog picks up a scent, it's just a matter of a few short seconds. The dog can lose the scent, thus causing the dog to start all over.

"Man what a miserable night. Not even a star is in sight. What I wouldn't give for a big bowl of parched peanuts and sitting by a big fire place wrapped in a big homemade quilt watching a good basketball game on the T.V," Little George whispers to Judy.

Turning his head around and gazing at Judy with his head light Little George notices her giving him her best poor little boy look. Then she replies in a glumly voice, "It's a good thing you don't ask for much Little George."

It takes Lady fifteen minutes to tree her first raccoon.

After the confirmation is completed by the timer and the two counters Lady is off on another trail.

For the most part the woods around Soap Stone are new growth pine trees with a hint of old hard wood stands mixed in. But the good thing about the woods is. They are not over-grown with brambles and bushes. Sometimes you have to run up a slight incline, or go around a small oxbow. But the footing is good solid ground.

"I can hear Lady barking down in a slew that runs off in the direction of Red Bluff," Judy yells out into the cold night air.

After a ten minute foot race Little George reaches the tree Lady is tapping. "Good girl. You got another one."

Looking around at everyone as they arrive to confirm his call of Treed Little George notices one of the counters is missing. Leaning close to Judy's ear he whispers so no one can hear him, "I guess we ran to fast and we lost someone?"

Mr. Ark Longtree their timer speaks up, "Old Pete Willow pulled up lame after he stumbled into a stump hole back there. So I told him to head on back to the starting line and get that ankle looked at. But I think we completed the necessary run for this tryout Little George. Let's head on back to the starting line for now."

Taking their time and walking a short distant behind their timer and counter Little George leans over and ask Judy, "Did you see Mr. Willow fall in a stump hole?"

"No I didn't. And the funny thing is. I don't even see any stump holes around here."

"That's what I'm talking about," Little George replies softly.

CHAPTER 70

Gracie ask, "What's got in to you tonight Old Man?"

"I keep thing about what we found in Old Hoy. And not knowing all the players involved in this drug ring is starting to get to me, especially when our grandson and Judy might have some unknown people following them around trying to kill Lady and maybe them too. All because they know Lady can identify these Knot Heads."

"Well if you're that worried about them. Why don't you and I load up a couple of twelve gage shotguns and take a little ride out to Soap Stone and do a little investigating of our own. Who knows what we might find?"

Giving Gracie a wink Big George says, "That's why I fell in love with you Gracie."

Giving Big George a surprise look Gracie says, "Why I thought you said you married me for my money Old Man."

"Well that to. But I knew you could shot and clean the game you killed and you could cook it too. And there was love involved too."

After loading the two shot guns and themselves into George Junior's nineteen-fifty red and white Chevrolet truck. Big George backs up the truck and shifts into first gear and heads the truck down the driveway.

Bouncing over the wooden cattle guard Big George pulls on the steering wheel and turns the truck left.

After a ride of a mile down Cherry Grove Road he turns onto Highway Twenty-Six. All the while he's shifting the truck into third gear.

Gazing at Gracie seated by the passenger's side door Big George ask, "When was the last time you was in Soap Stone Gracie?"

Looking over at Big George seated behind the steering wheel with a big Opossum Grin on his face and his big left arm resting on the open window frame Gracie says, "I don't really know, but if I had to guess. I'd have to count all my fingers, then take my shoes off and count all my toes."

Passing through Grant and heading north Big George and Gracie both know they're getting close. "I believe I see a bunch of truck lights and lantern lights in William Carr's hay field Grace. So I guess this is the place we're looking for?"

"I believe your right Old Man. Park over behind your truck and I'll go set in it. And you can walk over to the hay wagon and nose around while I keep a watch out for trouble."

"Sounds like a winner to me. Now don't shoot anybody unless you have to," Big George mutters.

"Don't worry about a thing Davy Crockett."

CHAPTER 71

Unseen by Big George and Gracie at the time is a man standing in the night shadows. The man is the tall stranger, who brought Lady to the clinic on that faithful day. A tall slim built man by the name of Carl Lopper. Somehow he's managed to fake a need to fill a prescription to get away from his cohorts in crime.

His other two running mates in crime are a two time loser just out of Angola State Prison by the name of Sam Puller.

Carl Lopper the tall stranger sometimes uses the name of Gabe among other alias depending on which side of the border he's operating.

The other man is Luke Holiday a short stocky barrel chested man from Lake Charles.

Carl's mission tonight is to leave a note in the kid's truck explaining everything that's happened so far and how sorry he is for shooting the dog.

After placing the note on the dash board Carl spots a truck pulling in. And the face he gets a glance of is none other than Doctor George. The same man he carried the dog to after he shot the dog in Old Hoy.

As he stays in the shadows, he spies a little old lady dressed in a light blue calico dress with a green cap on her head. And she's carrying a large gun over her shoulder. And the big man has a gun with him too.

As the big man walks toward a group of men, the little lady climbs up inside the kid's truck. After a few minutes of standing in the shadows Carl watches in complete surprise as a group of men start walking in his direction.

Thinking he's done all he can Carl makes a run for his truck. Pulling the door open he plops down onto the seat and inserts the key into the ignition.

Giving the key a twist the big V-8 roars to life. Pushing the clutch in and pulling the Floor Shifter back into first. Carl lets off the clutch with his left foot and presses down on the accelerator all the way to the Floor Board with his right foot.

In a matter of a few short seconds the truck is Fish Tailing down the black asphalt road leaving a scent of burnt rubber. A mile further down the road Carl turns on the truck head lights.

CHAPTER 72

"Well...well, I've never seen so many over the hill people in one place in all my life like I'm seeing right now," Big George says with a big belly laugh.

"Look who's calling the kettle black Dad-Burn-it," A voice shouts out.

"Over the hill, why Big George is almost down in the valley," Another voice yells out.

"Why give him a few more years and he'll be ready for that long Dirt Nap," Someone says.

"Dirt Nap hell... he's older then dirt," Farley said.

"Ok...ok. I know when I'm whipped. The real reason I'm here is I believe there might be a couple of Jelly Heads hanging around these parts. And they might try to hurt my grandson and Judy while trying to kill my grandson's dog."

After everyone settles down Big George tells everybody about the drug runners. And what happened in Old Hoy, leaving nothing out.

Tom Hurly walks up to Big George and says, "I've seen a man at different times standing around, or sitting in a new up pickup truck with four wheel drive. And I know for a fact he's not from around these parts. And when Little George and Judy left Mittie last week I noticed a different man in a different truck leave at the same time as they did. But at the time I didn't think nothing was a miss. You know how people come and go all the time at these try-outs."

Scratching the back of his neck Big George replies, "That could be one of the Jelly Heads, who got away from the sheriff and his deputy's out in Old Hoy a couple of weeks back?"

A voice in the back of the group of men shouts out, "Why I just seen that man a few minutes ago standing by the truck you just described."

"Hell… let's find that bird and ask him what in the "Sam Hill"' is he doing around here," Old man Tate says.

Huffing and puffing Big George stops and sucks in a lung full of air before he can speak, "You ok Gracie?" He chokes out.

"I'm fine. And I got a good look at that man. And I also had a good aim on that truck he's in. But I spied a group of people coming out the woods. And the funny thing is I found a piece of paper on the dash board with some writing on it when I got in the truck."

After adjusting his glasses and reading the note under the glare of truck head lights Big George says, "I need to show this to Sheriff Thomas."

Turning around and looking in the direction of the woods Big George says, "It looks like Little George and Judy with Lady and the men are coming out of the woods."

Once everything settles down and Mr. Farley makes his announcements of the winners.

Little George got a first place again.

After the announcement and the congratulations are over

Little George loads up Judy and Lady and heads for Judy's house.

His Grandpa George and Grandma Gracie are following close behind them.

Little George grumbles, "All this mystery is about to get to me."

Judy gazes over at Little George in the reflection of the headlights beams shinning behind them and says, "All I know is I'm scared to death."

CHAPTER 73

Driving over Carpenters Bridge, which spans the Whisky Chitto Creek, Little George slows down to get a better look at a camp site someone has placed on a big sand bar.

A big camp fire is blazing brightly and lighting up the surrounding water. From up high Little George and Judy can see people walking around. And someone is trying to row a canoe against the cold dark current.

While watching all this happening Little George says, "Well there's a Knot Head with nothing better to do at night."

Judy slides over closer to Little George's side to get a better view. In a second Little George can feel Judies body heat through her blue jeans as her thigh touch his leg.

"From up here the guy in the canoe looks like Emory Johnson," Judy replies.

For no reason Little George says, "I better get you home."

This is the first time Judy and Little George have every

touched. And they both realized it. His face turns red and Judy just smiles at him.

After walking Judy up to the front porch steps Little George notices a movement behind a curtain. And the porch light comes on. "I guess mother stayed up waiting for me," Judy says.

Tuning around and heading back for the truck Little George says, "See you Monday at school."

On his way home he's taking his time. Little George has so many feeling rushing through his mind. That he doesn't know where to start. Let alone how to handle them.

The feeling of losing his parents and his twin sister coupled with the loss of his leg. Along with his inability to play basketball a sport he dearly loves is a mood changer for him.

And learning to love the grandparents, who love him back unconditionally and now the love of a dog who gives him all her love and does everything he ask of her to do.

Now this deep feeling he has for Judy is starting to grow. How on earth can a person sort all these feelings out is a mystery to him. Seeing the lights up on the hill Little George knows he's almost home.

Driving up the driveway leading to his grandparent's home he lets out a sigh of relief and Lady gave out a soft moan.

Patting Lady on the head Little George whispers to her, "You did a great job tonight girl. After we eat I'll give you a good rub down."

CHAPTER 74

After a round robin of planning and talking to the sheriff over the phone it's agreed Little George will drive his father's truck and Grandpa George and Grandma Gracie will drive his red truck to the final Grand Championship. It will be a perfect ruse to fool the drug runners and bring them out of hiding. And the best part of all this planning is they have a week off to get ready.

Sunday morning comes and Sammy works his magic again. Listening to a couple of minutes of his high pitch crowing at 5:00 in the mourning makes you wonder. Can a rooster catch Laryngitis?

CHAPTER 75

After Little George's morning ritual in the bathroom he hobbles into the kitchen and plops down to a plate of French toast with powdered sugar and cinnamon sprinkled on top.

Gazing at Grandpa George seated at the head of the table Little George can see his grandpa's brow has a deep furrow. And he has his red, white, and blue patriot eyes this morning, which means he and grandma got very little sleep last night. Little George figures the best way to dig around in Grandpa George's mind is to wait till after breakfast.

After helping Grandma Gracie clear the kitchen table Little George walks out the back door and makes his way to the big barn next to the tool shed. His daddy's nineteen fifty Chevrolet pickup truck is setting in there just like a brand new truck right off the show room floor.

After a few short seconds Little George spies his Grandpa George standing in the shadows behind his Red International Harvester Tractor. "What do you think?" Grandpa George ask with a grin.

"I don't know what to say. I never thought of ever driving this truck."

Unknown to Little George his Grandpa George walked out ahead of him and was waiting for him in the shadows.

"You'll do more than just drive it Little George. It's yours for as long as you want it. I know your father would have wanted you to have it."

Little George can feel a slight sting sensation building up behind his eyes. And his throat feels tight and dry as he stammers, "I don't know what to say."

"Why don't we load up and head to church in your truck," Grandpa George says.

CHAPTER 76

After parking his truck and helping Grandma Gracie up the steps of the church Little George stays back talking to all his friends and kin folks. After a while he spies Judy all dressed up in a white dress with pink roses around the collar.

Looking Little George in the eyes Judy says with a big smile, "I see you're driving your father's truck now."

Feeling his face turning red Little George replies, "Grandpa and Grandma must of figured I'm matured enough to take care of it."

Gazing at Judy and the way the sun shines on her face Little George clears his throat and looking into Judy's emerald green eyes he ask, "Oh by the way. What are you doing after church?"

Looking up at the sky and humming to herself playing for all the time she needs before giving Little George an answer Judy finally says, "I guess nothing that can't wait... why?"

"I have something I'd like to show you that's very special. Maybe after church I can pick you up and we can spend some time together," Little George replies.

"Ok… but give me enough time to eat and get out of these clothes and into my jeans."

On the drive back home after church Little George senses his grandparents wants to ask him a question. But nether knows which one should ask him, or how to go about asking him. So Little George decides to answer the question before one of them can ask. "After dinner I'm going to take a little run over to "Carpenters Bridge"' and pickup Judy for a little walk along "Flat Creek"' this afternoon, if it's ok with you all?"

Grandpa George is the first to answer, "Oh--- that's a great idea," He says looking at Grandma Gracie

"Yes--- a walk in the wood after a big dinner is a good way to help your digestion."

After waiting for Judy to change into her everyday jeans Little George takes his time driving back to his grandparent's house.

"This must be something very special," Judy says with a big smile on her face.

Giving Judy his best poker face Little George replies, "It's a very important place and I think you'll find it very interesting."

CHAPTER 77

Afta a twenty minute walk into the woods Judy says, "Ok... here we are walking in the woods with Lady sniffing the ground. And you're sweating like you've run a country mile and it's a fifty degree day."

"I probability have too much cloths on. Besides I want to show you something very special to me. It's just a little ways further."

Walking through the dry winter leaves laying on the forest floor Little George knows they sound like a company of solders marching off to war. Even the animals know they're coming and have plenty of time to scurry out of their way.

Lady seems to be enjoying her afternoon walk. As they round the back forty acres they're welcomed by the sight of a mother deer and her fawn grazing on new spring grass.

A little further down a family of Blue Jays are in a Black Jack tree starting up a ruckus, which can be heard all over the woods.

"Here we are. Let me bend these branches out of the way," Little George says proudly.

With a puzzled look in her eyes Judy looks at Little George and says, "Why it's a Hickory Tree Little George."

"It's not just the tree I want to show you. It's what's carved on the side of it," Little George says as he grabs Judy's hand.

After they're through the branches Little George points to the names carved into the side of the big tree. "This is what I want to show you."

Little George can see the surprised look in Judy's eyes as she says, "Wow…I can remember hearing my daddy telling me about some of these folks of long ago."

"All of the names you see are people I'm related to, starting with my Great Grandparents all the way to my parents."

Amazed at the sight of the carved names Judy slowly and gently ran her hand over the carving as if she might break the letters. After a short minute, or two Judy turns to Little George and ask, "Do you think one day your name and mine might be on this tree?"

Losing his breath at hearing these words and turning beet red in the face Little George stammers, "That would be great."

On their walk back home Little George and Judy hold hands and Lady stays by their side. Every now and then Lady looks up at Little George and wiggle her tail ninety miles an hour as if she's giving him her approval.

CHAPTER 78

The last few days before the final Grand-Nite-Championship run Judy, Lady, and Little George spend all their free time with Sheriff Thomas and a few undercover deputies from Texas and Louisiana.

The plan is to let Grandpa George and Grandma Gracie be the decoys. And drive the red truck the drug gang has always seem Judy and Little George riding in. And Little George will take his father's truck and continue on with the Championship.

After their twelfth run through on what to do, the sun is starting to fade in the west.

"Ok folks does everyone know their call signs?" Sheriff Thomas ask.

"Judy and I will be High Test,"

"And Gracie and I are the Over the Hill Gang,"

Looking at his wrist watch and up at the darkening sky the sheriff says, "We'll meet up at the turnoff on Highway Twenty Six at 6:30 tomorrow evening sharp.

Then we'll let Big George and Gracie go in first and we'll follow right behind them. After that we'll split up just before the cattle guard in front the old gym. And Little George and Judy will drive in and head for the hay wagon before anybody's the wiser."

After they break the meeting up and everyone goes home. Little George takes Judy back home in his daddy's truck. On the drive to Judy's house neither one says a word for five miles. Finally Little George builds up the courage to ask Judy, "Are you scared?"

Looking down at her hands cupped in her lap Judy replies, "I'm just scared those crooks get away and they never catch them."

Little George looks at Judy and says, "Not to change the subject but did you mean what you said the other day under the hickory tree?"

Reaching over with her long arm Judy claps Little George on his shoulder. And with an embarrassing grin on her face she says, "Why yes I did. What about you?"

"I think it's the greatest thing in the world you and me being girlfriend and boyfriend."

CHAPTER 79

Grandpa George and Little George make their Saturday morning run to the clinic and check on a dog Grandpa George had performed an operation on the day before.

While there they also did the feeding and watering while Lady did her checking up on all the animals.

Little George has a feeling his Grandpa has a lot on his mind and he wonders what can it be.

Putting his big arm around Little George's shoulder Grandpa George leans over and says, "What do you say we take a break in my office?"

Lady follows behind Grandpa George and Little George with her eyes on both.

Little George knows Lady has a knack for sensing a person's body language, or their tone of voice.

"I'm starting to wish the Grand-Nite- Championship are over with and those drug runners are in jail," Little George says.

Setting in his black office chair with his feet propped

up on the corner of the desk Grandpa George replies smugly, "Before the sun comes up tomorrow morning the jail house in Oberlin will have a few more guest."

"I sure hope so. They know how to run fast and where to hide. It makes me wonder how they do it."

"It's a big operation Little George. Bigger then you and I want to know about. But that's not what I want to talk about."

In the dim light of the office lamp Little George can see a tear welling up in his Grandpa's eyes. At first glance this puzzles him. Then it occurs to Little George what his Grandpa might say will break his heart. Even Lady senses the sad mood that envelopes the room.

After collecting his thoughts Grandpa George starts to outline his hopes for Little George and the rest of his life.

"So... you see Little George the plan your daddy and I had was. When I retired the clinic would be his. Now that's impossible with him gone, and no one left in the family but you. So I guess what I'm asking you is. What are your plans after you graduate high school?"

Looking up at the white tile ceiling and trying to collect his thought's Little George says, "The thought of going to college and trying for a spot on the veterinarian medical school has kept me awake at nights. I know it want be easy. But I guess the love of animals must run deep in the family and I think Lady would like that too."

Without looking at his Grandpa George, Little George can tell by the sound of sucking in a big gulp of air he's said the right thing.

Maybe all of his Grandpa George's dreams might come true after all. Even though Little George knows in his heart he'll never replace his son.

"That's the best news I've heard in a long time. Why I believe I still know a few professors over at L.S.U. Maybe I can pull a few strings. A little help never hurt anybody," Grandpa George says with a big grin.

CHAPTER 80

Grant

The sun is in its final stages of the end of the day. And just like clockwork Sheriff Thomas and the undercover detectives are waiting for Grandma Gracie and Grandpa George and Little George, Judy and Lady at the Grant WYE. "Looks like a lot of serous people with big guns on their hips," Judy says.

"I'll take your word on that. I just hope no one gets hurt and this thing hurries up and gets over with so we can go back to a normal way of life," Little George replies.

After a brief run through on what everybody's dos and don'ts are they're ready to get started.

From the WYE to Grant is about a four mile ride. After you cross the concrete bridge that spans the "Whisky Chitto Creek.'" You can throw a rock and almost hit the Fairview High School Gym that was built in the early twenty's.

Turning right and parking next to the gym Little George reaches for the knob and douses the truck head lights. The first thing to catch his eyes are ten 55 gallon steel barrels all blazing with fire for heat and light. And around each barrel is a cluster of men and dogs surrounding the barrels trying to keep warm.

"My lord, would you just look at that pile of human bodies," Judy says pointing her finger in the direction of the barrels.

"That's what I'm staring at. I didn't know we had this many people living in Allen Parish."

The night air has a hint of ice in the air and every time a person talks you can see a hazy gray vapor swirl up out of their months and disappear. Even when the dogs bark, or howl, you see the same affect.

Pulling on his cotton cloves and buttoning his coat up Little George says, "I guess we better high tail it to the wagon and sign in. And pull our starting number. Then get in place were we can be seen."

"Lady and I are right behind you."

On their way around the gym Lady suddenly stops in her tracks and starts a low growing sound deep down in her throat. And the hair on her head and neck stands straight up.

"What's got into Lady tonight?" Judy says.

"I don't know, but if I had to bet I'd say she's picked up a scent she doesn't like. And it's probably one of the drug runners lurking around here."

CHAPTER 81

"Ok ...old eagle eyes. Where are the kids?" Gracie asked looking at Big George as he douse the truck headlights.

"I lost them when they walked around the gym. I guess they're headed for the check-in-wagon?"

"I sure hope Sheriff Thomas and his deputies are in place, or this plan is going to fail," Gracie mutters.

After a few minute of quiet time, the radio comes alive with the cracking voice of a deputy saying he's spotted three men following Little George, Judy, and Lady around the gym.

Sheriff Thomas's voice comes on the radio asking the deputy to follow close by and see if he can spot any indication the three men may be carrying weapons.

"That's it Gracie. I'm getting out of this truck and find out what those three "Jelly Heads'" are doing following our kids," Big George says as he pulls on the truck door handle.

Reaching over with both hands Gracie grabs a hand hold on Big George's coat collar. "No—no stay in this truck George. Don't you go balling into something you haven't a clue about? Let Sheriff Thomas and his people handle this. It's their show."

After three long minutes the radio buzzes to life again. This time a deputy reports the three men have separated.

The one with a dark blue coat jumped a fence and disappeared into the night. And the short bow legged one was seen headed for one of the fire barrels.

But the tall man dressed in white sweat shirt was last seen heading for a red International pickup truck parked by the F.F.A building.

"Look out the side door mirror Gracie and tell me what you see," Big George whispers.

Setting up straight and adjusting her granny glasses Gracie says in a surprised voice, "There's a tall skinny man in some kind of white shirt heading this away with something in his right hand. Oh no! It can't be George. I believe he has a big knife, or something in his right hand."

Hearing his wife saying these words Big George slides his left hand down between the door and the seat and pulls up a three foot piece of round hickory wood. "Well I got something right here for Mr. Stranger."

Startled by the sight of the club in Big George's hands Gracie says, "What on earth are you going to do with that "Billy Club,"' Old Man?"

"Oh--- I just thought I'd give Mr. Stranger a wood shampoo with my new club Gracie. After all he's the dirty rotten "Knot Head"' that shot Lady and now he thinks he's coming over here to hurt our grandson and little Judy. Hold down the fort. I'll be back in a few minutes."

Before Gracie can say another word Big George is out the door. Within a short second Gracie hears a wild blood curding scream and a loud thump that shakes the truck. "George don't you kill that man!!" Gracie shouts out.

From out of the dark Sheriff Thomas and two big burly deputies materialize with their guns drawn and beads of sweat shinning on their forehead. "OPPS," Sheriff Thomas said as he looks down at the man in the white sweat shirt rolling around on the ground holding his head and moaning. "Looks like the man ran into a Hickory Tree Big George."

"Umm-humm...I thought I'd let him have a little wood shampoo upside the head for what he did to Lady."

"Is anyone watching the kids?" Gracie says rounding the back of the truck carrying a twelve gage shotgun in her hands.

"I have two of my best deputies stationed in the woods, alone with the two counters and the timer," Sheriff Thomas replies.

"What about the other two "Jelly Heads?"' Big George ask.

"We arrested the short bow legged one as soon as he got to the fire barrels. He has a warrant out of Houston, Texas for drugs and a shooting.

Now this guy that's lying on the ground moaning with a knot on the side of his head has warrants out on him from Texas and Louisiana."

"What about the one in the dark blue coat?" Big George ask.

"From what I've been able to find out about him he's

wanted by other law enforcement agents. They seem to think he's the ring leader of a big drug gang out of Huston. And they believe this is the gang that's been running drugs out of Mexico and into the U.S.A. Now we have him here in Louisiana establishing grow gardens of marijuana right here in Old Hoy. And they want this fella real bad and we want him too"

"Do you think we need to head into the woods and arrest this man before he hurts someone sheriff?" Gracie ask with a concerned voice.

"Let's just wait a little bit Gracie. I don't need a bunch of people in the woods with guns stumbling around in the dark. Let's give the deputies a chance at this bird. I want them to catch this man here in Louisiana so I can charge him with a crime. Then put his butt behind bars at Angola State Prison for good."

CHAPTER 82

"Did you hear that Judy?" Little George whispered

"No I didn't hear a thing Little George."

After everyone crosses the fence and walks a short distance Mr. Odom stops and calls everyone to come close to him. "Judy, Little George these three men are under cover deputies with the sheriff's office. They seem to think we might have a criminal out here in the woods trying to kill Lady and possibly do bodily harm to both of you."

"We have a hunch we're in danger Mr. Odom. We're working with the Sheriff too," Little George says.

"I had a hunch you two were in on it. Ok everybody find a spot and set down and keep real quiet. And keep your head lights off and your ears open. Things might get a little dicey in a short," Mr. Odom said.

Setting in the dark in the middle of the woods with three men a girl and a three legged dog waiting for a killer to appear is not one of Little George's favorite things to be doing.

The only light they have comes from the stars when the heavy clouds move away for a few seconds. And the only sound's their ears pickup is their heart beating.

Lady has her head on Little George's left leg and at times she takes in a deep breath. After a short minute of her doing this she all of a sudden stops. And now Little George can hear a deep growling noise deep in her throat.

Without warning Lady springs up and make's one giant leap up over Little George's head and into the bushes behind him. In an instant a blood curdling scream is heard and two large deputies come rushing through the bushes.

Little George reaches out in the dark and grabs Judy by the arm and both run for a big pine tree to hide behind. But Mr. Odom beat both to the tree.

Within a second there are at least a half a dozen people running towards them.

After a few minutes of shouting and mumbling and cursing, alone with the noises of men rolling around on the ground and branches braking. The noise finally settles down.

Now Little George hears his Grandpa George's voice calling out, "Little George, Judy where are you?"

Stepping out from behind the pine tree Little George turns on his head light and shouts out, "We're over here Grandpa."

As Little George steps out from around the tree. The next thing Little George feels is a cold wet nose touching his hand. "There you are girl," Little George says as Lady brushes his leg.

Once the deputies have their man in handcuffs and everyone's caught their breaths. Mr. Odom walks over to Judy and Little George and says, "You two feel like getting started. I believe all the excitement is over for now."

Little George gazes at Judy and Lady. "I guess so Mr.

Odom. What else can happen?"

As soon as the rules are read and the interdictions are done. Everyone enters the woods and Lady takes off like a road-runner. It takes her just seven minutes to tree her first Raccoon. After a short break to compare notes Little George lets Lady lose with a. "Find them girl, tree that raccoon, go find them."

Mr. Odom walks up to Little George shaking his head. "Little George you sure Lady isn't more human than dog?"

Gazing at Mr. Odom in the dim light Little George spies a grin on Mr. Odom's face. "I'm not all that certain Mr. Odom. But sometimes I think she can read a person's mind."

In a matter of forty five minutes Lady has treed four raccoons. After a short break Mr. Odom calls everyone together, "Will gents that's a record in my life time. I remember hearing of a dog treeing three raccoons. But I've never heard of a dog tree-ing four. If all agree, let's call this run completed and let's head on in."

After three hour of standing in the cold damp night air the tryouts are finally over. Now it's just a matter of time till they find out who will be this year's Grand-Nite-Champion. "I wish they would hurry up my toes are frozen," Judy says as she stomps her feet on the cold ground.

"Here comes Mr. Farley now," Little George says.

Climbing up the old rickety steps onto the hay wagon and walking to the center. Mr. Farley raises both of his arms up into the air and proceeds to clear his throat for a few seconds before starting. "Ok folks… I'll make this short and sweet like a jackasses walk. Here we go. In fourth place I have Mr. Tom Hurly." After the announcement a small applause can be heard and a couple of cow horns sound off.

"Ok folks… now a little quite please."

"And here we have Mr. Ty Sam coming in with a strong third place showing." Again a round of cheers goes up and a couple of "Blue Tick Hounds'" starts howling and a "Red Bone Hound'" chimes in.

"All right folks we're getting close," Mr. Farley said as he tries to adjust his glasses to read the ballots in the dim light.

"Here now folks we have Mr. Slim Nugget coming in at a respectable second place finish." A rousing cheer goes up and echoes through the woods for three minutes.

"I'm about to have a heart attack. Why does Mr. Farley drag it out for so long?" Judy mutters.

Before Little George can answer Judy, It dawns on him he's holding Judy's hand and Lady is looking up at him. Feeling his face getting warm Little George replies, "I don't have a clue, but he does this all the time. Sometimes I get the idea he's practicing for a political speech."

As the crowd quiets down Mr. Farley shouts out, "OK now folks this is the one everyone's been waiting for."

After a moment of silent and a few short seconds of clearing his throat Mr. Farley musters up his fineness statesmanship voice, "And now this year's winner of The Grand-Nite-Championship is none other than that young man out of The Flat Creek Community--- Little George and his "Chesapeake Bay Retriever'" Lady, alone with his assistant Miss Judy Long."

All at once a concerto of barking, truck horns blowing and cow horns sounding off can be heard. And voices yelling out at the top of their lungs are saying, "I knew you two could do it, Atta-a-boy Little George." And a sweet little voice in the front of the crowd can be heard yelling, "Atta-Girl Judy, You did-it." Looking in the direction of the voice Little George spies his Grandma Gracie waving a white handkerchief.

As the cheering subsides and the slaps on the shoulders stops, Little George turns towards Judy and says, "Thanks for helping me with Lady. Without your help I couldn't have won."

CHAPTER 83

Two weeks has pasted since the night they won the Grand-Nite-Championship. And Sheriff Thomas decides to drive out to Big George's house to fill him in on the missing pieces of what happened at Grant.

Setting at the big kitchen table with a cup of coffee in his hand Sheriff Thomas says, "Well folks this case has as many twists and turns as a "Blue Runner Snake,"

Gazing at Sheriff Thomas seated across the table Big George replies, "Well for one thing I'm still dazed and confused about these three drug runners."

After taking a pull on his coffee mug Sheriff Thomas says, "I know what you mean George. Maybe I can shed some light on the subject."

Gazing at Sheriff Thomas, Gracie says with a knowing smile, "I'm all ears sheriff.

Sheriff Thomas looks at Gracie, as he says, "Ok... for starters Mr. Carl Lopper was trying to warn Little George and Judy of the impending danger from Luke Holiday and his running mate Mr. Sam Puller. But in the end he ended up with a Wood Shampoo."

"That Wood Shampoo was for what he did to Lady," Big George replies with a big smile on his face.

"Sheriff Thomas what about Mr. Pete Willow? Judy and I never seen him fall in a stump hole, but he did go a miss," Little George ask.

After a short chuckle Sheriff Thomas says, "Mr. Willow is an undercover detective working for me. At the time when he disappeared on you we had a report that Link Noah was seen in the area. So we searched the woods and the roads, but came up empty handed."

"Well that explains that mystery," Little George says.

"Now that most of the people involved in this drug operation are either already in jail, or on the run. I have one more case I need to wipe off my list," Sheriff Thomas Says.

Little George gazes at Sheriff Thomas as he ask, "Would that case possibly involve the Noah's?"

Setting his coffee mug on the kitchen table Sheriff Thomas says in a matter-of-fact voice, "You hit the nail right on the head Little George."

"Those two "Knot Heads" have grown into living legends around here," Gracie says.

Standing up and pushing his chair back in place Sheriff Thomas replies, "Well folks. I'm planning on making those two legends the last of the Moon Shine Legends."

Standing up Big George clasps the sheriff's right hand. "If you need our help don't hesitate to call."

"I'll remember the offer George. And thank you for your help and tell Lady thanks you for me," Sheriff Thomas says looking at Little George.

After Sheriff Thomas drives out onto the Cherry Grove Road. Big George stands on the front porch with Gracie and Little George watching a brown plum of dust swirling up into the air. As the sheriff drives down the road headed for Highway Twenty-Six. "I believe we just might see the good sheriff again," Big George says.

CHAPTER 84

After the arrest and jailing of Sam Puller, Luke Holiday, and Carl Lopper Sheriff Thomas realizes the case of the "Old Hoy" Drug Runners is bigger than anybody had expected.

With the help of Carl Lopper's confession law enforcement agents from Louisiana and Texas start one of the largest drug round up's in history. After it's all said and done with. There are over one hundred people arrested.

The first raid is conducted in and around the small southern Texas settlement of "Whoop," Texas. With the location of "Whoop" being on the north shore of the Rio Grande. It makes it easy to transport the American grown Marijuana into Mexico and exchange it for Mexican Cocaine.

After the exchange is completed the drug runners start a run through a dozen small towns in a dozen Texas counties. Once they arrive at the Louisiana State line. It's just a matter of crossing the Sabine River at Many, Louisiana.

Once in Louisiana it becomes a wild run through the piney woods, which are known by the locals as the "Big Sticks.'"

For the most part the cars and trucks used in these runs are designed to run on black top roads, or gravel roads. The front wheels of the cars are designed to flop on a sharp curve, thus giving the driver a sharper turning radius to elude close run ends with pursuing cops. And the "Fire Lines'" in the woods come in handy as a getaway route.

The sophistication of this organization is mind boggling to law enforcement. Even the use of "Cooling off Houses'" is used. And some homes are used as "Duck and Hide Houses.'" In a close chase the garage doors are left open and the drug runner will simple drive into the garage and douses the car lights. And the garage door closes leaving the cops in the dark.

Everything is so well synchronized from start to finish. That should a runner be more than ten minutes late checking in at designated spot. The whole organization will disengage and go into a forty-eight hour cooling off period. When the drug runner doesn't show up on time and the news doesn't carry information on the T.V., or the radio. People called Seekers will go out and retrace the runner's rout trying to find him.

The more Carl talks, the more law enforcement are amazed at the suffocation and size of the drug operation.

The one thing that stands up for Carl is the fact he tried to warn Little George and Judy of the impending danger. And he voiced his remorse for having shot Lady.

Now next on Sheriff Thomas's list of things to do is arrest Mars and Link Noah. It seems every time he's made a push against the Noah's. They would simple fade away. But now with Carl's information on the Vietnam "Geophones'" Mars salted the woods with. He now has a new plan in the making.

"So tell me Carl. Old Mars is using these "Army Geophones'" to hear people driving, or walking close to his shack. Or approaching his Moonshine Still?" Sheriff Thomas ask.

Dressed in black and white striped jail house clothes and handcuffs on both wrist Carl looks up at Sheriff Thomas and stammers, "Yes sir."

"Tell me Carl. How long was the bull dozer ride from Mars shack to his Moonshine Still?"

"I'm not too sure Sheriff. I was kind of busy hanging on to that dam Bulldozer. But if I had to guess, I'd say the ride was about four miles and the walk another mile give, or take a few feet."

Rubbing a three day old salt and pepper beard Sheriff Thomas has a feeling he has all the information Carl has, yet he needs just one more missing piece of the puzzle. "How was the Moonshine Still set up and how far from the creek was it?"

With his blood-shot eyes Carl gazes at Sheriff Thomas and mutters, "From what I remember the Moonshine Still sets about fifty yards from the creek. That way a person fishing can't see it through the trees."

In a calm voice Sheriff Thomas ask, "What about that hollowed out tree Link was in. Give me a description and location of it?"

"That dam fool Link! Why he almost killed us with that dam A.K.-47,"Carl blurts out.

"I know Carl. But I need to know about that tree."

Rubbing the sweat off his hands onto his jail house prisoner clothes Carl said, "It's not a real tree Sheriff. It's made to look like a White Oak stump with a couple of branches sticking out from the trunk."

"And the branches is where Link shot at you from?"

"Yes Sir," Carl replies.

After Carl is taken back to his cell Sheriff Thomas decides to call Big George. Picking up the receiver he punches Big George's number. On the second ring a voice on the other end of the line said, "Hello."

"This is Sheriff Thomas. What are you up too?"

"Oh...nothing much. What about you?" Big George replies.

"I just got through interrogating Carl Lopper and he's given me a lot of unknown information. But I may need your help connecting the dots."

Hearing this peaks Big George's interest. "I'll help you any way I can Sheriff."

"Thanks George...this case with the Noah's has grown to be a pain in the neck. But with your help and being born and raised in the woods, which surround Whisky Chitto Creek. You just might hold the key that will help me put old Mars and Link behind bars for good."

"If I got the key, I'll help you all I can,"

"Thanks George. It might be awhile before I can turn loose here and come over. But as soon as I can we'll meet and talk."

"Sounds like a winner to me. Just let me know when. And I'll have a pot of coffee on the stove."

CHAPTER 85

As the days turn into weeks and the weeks into months Sheriff Thomas finally has a chance to catch a breather.

The trials for the three drug runners are set to go. And he's put in a good word for Carl to Judge Ray Bean.

After a lot of consideration Judge Ray made a ruling to send Carl to a prison farm instead of Angola.

The F.B.I. have made their charges and the Texas Rangers are filing their charges. The last to file papers are The Interpol Police.

Walking over to his stainless steel coffee pot Sheriff Thomas runs a few scenarios over in his mind. First the big drug bust in Old Hoy was a god sent. And the total destruction of the multimillion dollar drug operation is a big satisfaction to his men and himself. Now it's the problem with the Noah's and their Moonshine business. Most of the evidence against the Noah's is just word of mouth on the streets.

Sheriff Thomas and a few of his deputies in the pass have tried to do a little recon in the area where they think the location of Mars Noah's Moonshine Still may be. But for the last three years nothing has panned out. It seems as though the mystery of just what Mars is doing back in the woods alone the Whisky Chitto Creek will remain a mystery for every.

But in the back of his mind he has to find a solution to this problem and lay it all to rest once and for all. Because the longer it goes without an end the harder it makes it on his family and himself.

CHAPTER 86

S heriff Daryl Thomas sets at his desk flipping a pencil between his thumb and forefinger. The only thing on his mind now is how can he arrest Mars and Link Noah without losing half of his deputies?

On the second telephone ring he picks up the receiver. "Allen Parish Sheriff Department, Sheriff Thomas speaking, how may I help you?"

The voice on the other end says, "Just checking in on you old law dog."

Getting caught off guard by the gravelly voice Sheriff Thomas barks out, "Look who's calling the pot black. Are you still holding down the fort in Calcasieu Parish?"

Letting out a soft chuckle, the voice replies, "Not hardly Daryl. I'm like the Little Dutch Boy with his finger in the in the dike."

"Too many leaks out there?" Sheriff Thomas laughs.

"You got it."

"What's the pleasure of me getting a phone call from

the high sheriff of Calcasieu Parish?"

"Oh... I just wanted to touch base with you. I heard through the grape vine the other day you got that drug gang under wraps?"

"Yep...most of the paper work is in. And the law enforcement agents have filed their paper work. Listen while I have you on the horn thanks for all your help Hank."

"Any time Daryl... any time. Well I better let you get back to work."

"Thinks for the call, but I still have one more case to close."

"Huh... I through you had all the loose ends nailed down."

"I do Hank, but I still have a father and son problem that's connected to the drug runners. Plus these two are in the Moonshine making business."

"Sounds like a couple of rough old boys," Sheriff Hank Banks says.

"Their rough as a Corn Cobb, but the big problem I'm having is where we think their Moonshine Still may be located."

After a moment of silences Sheriff Banks says, "Knowing some of the woods in Allen Parish from my deer hunting days. I'd say that Moonshine Still is probability back in the "Boon Docks.'"

Letting out a soft chuckle Sheriff Thomas replies, "You hit the nail on the head Hank. It's in the Boom Docks and then some. I could get to them. But I'd stand a chance of losing some good men."

Listening to Sheriff Thomas voice, Sheriff Banks can tell the sheriff of Allen Parish is at his wits end. "I understand your way of thinking Daryl. Nobody wants to lose a man no matter what."

"And there lies the problem. I've tried several times to find that Moonshine Still. But there's so much woods and creeks to deal with. There's no way to creep up on them. Let along find them."

"I know what you mean. Before we hang up let me give you the phone number of an old boy who's helped me out on a couple of tough cases."

"Hold up a minute while I get a "Scratch Pad" to write on."

After a little paper shuffling Sheriff Thomas comes back on the line and said, "Ok…shoot that number to me."

After giving the number Sheriff Banks says, "The old boys name is Hambone Jones. That's the only name he goes by."

Scratching the back of his neck Sheriff Thomas mutters, "Just what does Hambone do?"

"He flies a Piper L-4 Grasshopper airplane."

"Ok…and just what does this Grasshopper do. And how will it help me arrest these two knot heads?"

"With a little luck old Hambone might be able to fly over the spot where your Moonshiners are. And he can take a few photo that can give you an idea of how to get to them and arrest them."

Swing his long legs off the top of his desk Sheriff Thomas says, "You just might have something."

After hanging up the phone Sheriff Thomas stares at the phone for a short few minutes.

After running a few scenarios over in his mind he punches in the number Sheriff Banks gave him. On the fifth ring a high pitched voice answers, "Hold on a minute."

Looking at the clock hanging on the wall Sheriff Thomas figures a five minute wait is long enough.

Reaching over to hang up the phone he hears a voice say, "Hambone flying service… how can I help you?"

Placing the phone next to his ear Sheriff Thomas ask, "Is Mr. Hambone in?"

"Yes he is. And you're looking at him right now."

After that remark the sheriff has second thoughts about carrying on this conversation. But he says, "This is Sheriff Thomas of the Allen Parish Sheriff's Office. A little while ago I spoke to Sheriff Banks about a problem I'm having. And he recommended I talk to you about getting you to help me out."

"Yes…yes I know Sheriff Banks real well. I did a few flying jobs for him."

"Great Mr. Hambone, because I have a flying job I hope you can help me out with."

"Oh… If this person lives on this plant I can find him," Hambone said.

"When can we meet and talk things over?" Sheriff Thomas ask.

Humming for a few short seconds Hambone replies, "How about tomorrow morning say…oooh about nine-o-clock."

Looking at his daily planner Sheriff Thomas says, "That'll work for me. Now before we hang up where can I meet up with you?"

"When you come in on I-10, take the highway 14 exit south. Then take a left on Broad Street. And a little ways down on your right you'll see a little white greasy spoon restaurant called the Bombs-A-Way."

"See you then."

CHAPTER 87

The next morning is a bright and sunny day. Heading out of Oberlin on Highway 165 and passing rice fields, which are now emerald green Sheriff Thomas pushes his new squad car.

Most of the small towns nestled along the four lane highway are agriculture supported. With big rice Silos perched on the side of the railroad tracks.

Reaching I-10 Sheriff Thomas heads west towards Lake Charles. After a twenty minute drive he spots his turn off coming up.

Taking the highway 14 exit and over the overpass. It's a short drive to Broad Street.

Turning left and a couple of hundred years down on the right sits the world famous Bombs-a-Way. A relict left over from the days of The Lake Charles Air Force Base and The New Moon Drive Inn.

Walking through the double glass doors the first thing that hits a person is the odors of years of cooking Ham Burgers, French Fries, Eggs, and Bacon. Along with the strong black Chicory Coffee that kept the Airman awake on guard duty.

The black and white tile floor has seen its better days. And the short order cook standing behind the counter is dressed in all white pants, white tee shirt, and a white apron. This is usually a dead giveaway of a person that's just gotten out of jail.

"Hey... Sheriff Thomas, over here," A high pitched voice yells out.

Gazing in the direction of the voice Sheriff Thomas spies a middle age man with a slim built dressed in brown khaki pants, and a khaki shirt. And he has a brown leather jacket with multicolored insignias on the front and back. "Grab a seat and I'll get you a cup of oil," The man says.

Plopping down onto a corner booth seat Sheriff Thomas watches a man of about sixty years old with a weight of maybe one hundred and twenty pounds with a patch of light brown hair on his head.

CHAPTER 88

Hambone Jones A.K.A. Roy Jones is the last of the fly-by-the-seat of your pants pilots. Raised on a large rice farm in Southwest Louisiana, Roy Jones learned to fly while seating in his father's lap, as his father sprayed the rice fields in his yellow Ag. Cat-Airplane.

By the time Roy was in his early teens he was flying the airplane by himself. After graduating High School he joined the Air Force.

It was either join something at the age of eighteen, or wait and get drafted into the Army. And everybody knows what happens after Boot Camp, because the Vietnam War was going strong.

Once it's discovered Roy knows how to fly a plane. He's transferred to a flight school in Texas. Once he completes his training. Roy is sent to Vietnam where he flew an L-4 Grasshopper for four years.

After an eight year hitch in the Air Force, Roy heads back to the farm and the rice fields.

Then one day the sheriff of Calcasieu Parish called and asked if he could fly an airplane call a Grasshopper.

The nickname of Hambone comes from his father. The saying is, when Roy is flying his mouth is always moving like he's chewing on a Hambone, thus the name of Hambone was bestowed upon Roy.

Walking back to where Sheriff Thomas is seating Hambone ask, "How was the trip?"

Taking a pull on his cup of coffee Sheriff Thomas gazes at Hambone. "Fine Mr. Hambone."

With his forehead furrowed Hambone says, "From what you told me yesterday you're having a little problem with a few characters up your way."

Looking up from his cup of coffee Sheriff Thomas replies, "You could call Mars and his son Link characters Mr. Jones. But the truth of the matter is. Both of these men are dangerous and want blink an eye, when they shoot you."

Dumping a teaspoon of sugar into his cup Hambone cast an eye at Sheriff Thomas. "Well that being the case sheriff. I guess we need to get to work. Now just what is it you need me to do for you?"

"Sheriff Banks tells me you've done a little work for him using an airplane."

With a big grin slowly creasing his face Hambone replies, "Well I took a few pictures of some people and places, the sheriff was interested in."

"That's exactly what I need you to do for me."

"When do you need me to start sheriff?"

"As soon, as you can."

"Ok...that being the case can you send me the location and the information you want me to gather for you?" Hambone says as he sets his coffee cup back down.

"You got it. I'll have one of my deputies deliver everything to you first thing in the morning."

"That'll work sheriff."

On the drive back to his office in Oberlin, Sheriff Thomas hopes he can develop a plan to arrest Mars and Link Noah without getting some of his men killed, or shot up.

CHAPTER 89

Bright and early the next day Mr. Hambone has the paper work Sheriff Thomas promised in hand. Looking at the paper work Hambone hums a little tune. Then he looks at Deputy Lee. "Sounds like a couple of rough old boy's?"

Smiling back at Hambone Lee replies, "You might be nice and call them that. But some might call them other names."

Looking Lee in the eyes Hambone says, "Well I better get loaded up and start doing my job. From these reports there's no telling where that Moonshine Still is located."

Once the little L-4 Grasshopper is fueled up Hambone turns the little airplane on a heading of due north. After thirty minutes of flight time he can see the city of Kinder. And a little further north the town of Oberlin shows itself. Banking the Grasshopper a little to the left Hambone has the small airplane following Highway Twenty-Six heading due west.

Flying over the Calcasieu River and still following Highway Twenty Six. In a matter of a few short minutes the Whisky

Chitto Creek comes into view.

The slow moving current with the snow white sand bar's show an emerald green forest surrounding the creek. "Man what a sight," Hambone mumbles to himself.

Flying up stream Hambone hopes to fly over something he can identify as Mars Noah's home. And from there back track to the creek and find the sight of the Moonshine Still. Coming around a large bend in the creek Hambone spots a light gray haze in the air, or maybe a light fog coming off the cool water.

After thirty minutes of flying time. And making a dozen figure eights and taking twenty pictures. Hambone decides to head back to Lake Charles.

CHAPTER 90

After a week of flying day and night and keeping a time log on everything he's seen. The only problem Hambone has with his recon flights is the lush green forest that covers the Noah's land.

At times he can see Mars moving about and smoking a cigarette in broad daylight. Then at times nothing is moving and not a soul is in sight.

Hambone has finally decided to give Sheriff Thomas a call. And give him a run down on what he's seen so far. And the pictures he's taken.

"Sheriff I got those pictures you wanted. And the time frames which I've seen any movement from Mr. Mars, and Mr. Link. It's not much. But I hope it helps you out."

"That's the best news I've heard in a coons age Mr. Hambone. How about I meet you in the morning at the Bombs-Away and pick up the information."

"I'll have our booth reserved and a mug of oil waiting Sheriff."

"Sounds like a winner. See you in the morning."

CHAPTER 91

After picking up the big manila envelope from Hambone in Lake Charles Sheriff Thomas takes his time driving back to Oberlin. With a thousand thoughts racing through his mind he's tried placing the most important things first.

His family life in in shambles, but worth saving and the hours he's spent on the arrest of the drug runners is almost at an end.

Next on his agenda is the arrest and jailing of the Noah's.

After that's over its vacation time for him and his family, but first things first. Looking at the

Envelope lying on the passenger's seat Sheriff Thomas hopes these pictures helps put an end to the Noah's once and for all.

Passing through Kinder a drizzling rain starts to fall and dimpling the windshield. The rain is so light there's no need to put the wipers on.

Turning left at the intersection of Highway One Ninety and One Hundred Sixty Five. And around a corner sets the city jail. Parking his patrol car in front Sheriff Thomas slides out and walks in through the front doorway.

Chief Jerry Mack and Sheriff Thomas have known each other since their football playing days at Oberlin. Walking down the hallway Sheriff Thomas knocks on a light green colored door with a black name tag, which has white blocked lettering saying Chief of Police.

Opening the door slowly and sticking his head in. "I must be looking at the hardest working Lawman in Allen Parish."

Looking up from his paperwork Chief Mack replies, "I don't know about that. From the news I'm hearing. It's the Sheriff of Allen Parish that's the number one man."

"Don't believe all you read Jerry," Sheriff Thomas chuckles.

Standing up behind his desk Chief Mack extends his arm across the desk and clasps Sheriff Thomas right hand and pumps it up and down. "What brings the Sheriff of Allen Parish to Kinder?"

Setting down in a light gray metal chair and crossing his leg Sheriff Thomas replies, "I'm getting ready to make a push against the Noah's and I happen to remember you telling me a couple of months back you arrested an old boy with a trunk full of Moonshine here in Kinder."

Furrowing his brow in thought Chief Mack says, "Yea…It seems like the fella lived somewhere around a place called Soapstone. And the name he gave the patrolman was Link George."

Cracking a smile Sheriff Thomas replies, "You probably had Link Noah under arrest."

Giving Sheriff Thomas a surprised look Chief Mack says, "You mean they boot leg all the way down here too?"

Getting up from his chair Sheriff Thomas replies, "Yep…but I hope to put an end to it real soon."

On the ten mile drive back to Oberlin, Sheriff Thomas

hopes to end the Noah's reign of King of The Moonshiners real soon.

CHAPTER 92

The only loose ends to this case for Sheriff Thomas are the Noah's. Now that things are slowing down he's decided to take Big George up on that cup of coffee. Sliding onto the front seat of his squad car he heads west out of Oberlin on Highway Twenty Six.

Crossing the Calacasieu River Bridge he lets the car coast across to the other side. The clear water and snow white sand bars reminds him of better times when his wife and three children would camp out on the river.

All it took was a tent a fishing pole and a bunch of wieners and marshmallows to have a great time.

Eight miles further Sheriff Thomas spots the Veterinarian Clinic of Big George perched on a small knoll. Turning in the parking lot Sheriff Thomas parks his car by the front doors. Sliding out the driver's door and walking in through the front door. He spots Big George with his back to him standing at the receptions desk talking to a lady.

Sheriff Thomas walks up to Big George and says, "I'm a little late, but a good cup of coffee would go a long ways about now."

Turning around with a surprised look on his face Big George replies, "Well I can fix you right up with a big cup of coffee sheriff. Come on in my office where we can talk."

Taking a lone pull on his cup of coffee and setting it down on the corner of Big George's desk Sheriff Thomas says, "I'm sorry for being this late George. But this case was a monster and I felt I needed to stay with it till the end."

"No apology necessary sheriff," Big George replies as he puts his coffee cup down.

"Thinks... I appreciate that. I all so wanted to say thinks for all the help you and Little George, Judy, and Lady has given me."

"You're welcome. From what I've seen on the T.V. and heard on the local radio stations this grew into an international case."

"Yes Sir it did. The Feds are taking over the case now and Interpol is interested in parts of the case too."

"Wow... there must be some big fish in this pond?"

"They seem to think there is, but I still have an open case of my own. And it involves old man Mars and that boy of his Link. Both of them "Jelly Heads" were connected to the drug runners. And I want to bust that Moonshine Still of Mars and send him and Link up the river to Angola for a long stay."

Big George notices dark circles under both eyes of Sheriff Thomas, a sure sign of a man neglecting his sleep. "You mentioned something about maybe needing some help from me."

"Yep...that's right George. You were raised around these parts and you know the woods like the back of your hand."

"You might say that. I've walked these woods deer hunting, and squirrel hunting most all my life."

"I figured that. Here's what I've got from Carl Lopper.

The reason nobody's been able to shut down old Mars Moonshine Still is. He has listening devices planted all over the woods. So the only way I can figure out to get close enough to put those two down is to come through the back door of his operation."

"It just might be a mean battle if he knows you're coming," Big George says.

"You and I are on the same page George. I don't want to lose a man in this operation. That's why I don't want to go in through the front door."

"I get you now. You want me to help you find a way through the woods to get at that Moonshine Still and Mars and Link?"

"You got it George."

Folding his big arms across his chest Big George ask, "Ok. The next question I have is. When do you want to do this?"

"As soon, as possible.

Let me walk out to my car. I have a few pictures I'd like you to look at."

Returning back in a few short minutes to Big George's office the sheriff lays a black briefcase down on top Big George's desk. Snapping the two brass locks open he pulls out a brown envelope containing two strange pictures. One shows a daytime scene of some woods and a creek and the other is a nighttime scene.

Standing up from his chair Big George walks around the corner of his desk and looks down at the pictures the sheriff has spread out on his desk and ask, "What have you got there sheriff?"

"This first picture is a daytime picture taken by a pilot

working for the sheriff department in Lake Charles. He also went back and took this infrared night time picture I asked for. I'm thinking the area the picture is showing is right around where Carl said they were. If you look real close you can spot a small hazy gray spot in this daytime photo."

Straining his eyes Big George adjusted his glasses and says, "Oh... Yea I see it. What is it?"

"At first I thought it was a defect in the film. So I asked the pilot to make a night time run in his "Piper L-4 Grasshopper Airplane"' and take this Infrared photo. After we analyzed the photo we can see a hot image right there on that big bend of the creek."

Big George looks sideways at Sheriff Thomas and ask, "What kind of Grasshopper is that airplane?"

Laughing Sheriff Thomas repeats, "The Army calls it a Grasshopper and I believe it was used mostly for observation. When the Air Force closed down "The Lake Charles Air Force Base"' they gave the sheriff at that time this airplane. Then the sheriff gave it to a man by the name of Hambone Jones. From that time on the little plane has been used for a number of mission. The unique thing about this little airplane is that it can fly at a whopping eighty-five miles an hour. And that's slow enough to take good photos and it's quite enough not to be heard."

"So you believe this red and yellow glow by the creek could possibly be old Mars Moonshine Still?"

"I think it is George. But I need you to tell me where this location is on Whisky Chitto Creek," Sheriff Thomas said pointing at the picture.

Rubbing the back of his neck Big George remarks, "If I'm not wrong. I'd say what we're looking at is the Mill House Bend.

Gazing at the picture Sheriff Thomas says, "Well... that's a new one on me."

Letting out a small chuckle Big George says, "That name goes back to the first settlers, who settled around this area. They built a mill on the banks of the creek to grind their corn, maze, and other grains. They believed the current of the creek was fast enough to turn the big water wheel to do the job. But they didn't figure in the spring floods and the soft sand they built on."

"So the mill washed away?"

"Yep... but it stood for better than sixty years. And it taught the people not to build to close to the creek."

"I can certainly sympathize with the people. Now getting back to my little problem."

"Well...when I was a kid my grandfather and I hunted all over these woods around that area. And mostly we hunted ducks."

Looking at the daytime photo Sheriff Thomas says, "Ducks... I don't see a lake, or a pound. Where would you find ducks George?"

Looking at the sheriff with a big smile Big George replies, "Years back there was a lake across from The Mill House Bend, the old folks called it "The Old Grass Lake."' It seems that thousands of years ago the creek cut another channel that moved the creek bed a couple of hundred yards further south. But the water from the creek stayed in the old creek bed for years and the trees grew up around the banks of the lake. After a while the ducks started coming in at about sunset to eat the acorns that would fall into the water."

"Is the Grass Lake still there?"

"Not as it was Sheriff. About twenty years ago the

water level went down and the lake dried up."

"How can we use the lake to get to the Moonshine Still, now that the water gone?"

"I figure we can walk the lake bed unseen. Once we reach the end of the lake we'll be about seventy-five yards from the Moonshine Still. The only problem we have is. We'll be on the opposite side of the creek."

"That's not bad George. Tell you what. Give me a couple of weeks to work on a plan. And I think you and me and maybe Little George along with Lady just might make a Recon in there just to see how thing set before we make a big push. What do you think?"

"Let me know when," Big George says.

CHAPTER 93

Sheriff Thomas is setting at his desk in the dim light and gazing at a stack of papers waiting for his signature. He knows paper work is the last thing on his mind. His office window on the second floor of the Allen Parish Court House looks down on the main drag of Oberlin. And on one side of the big oval window stands the red, white, and blue flag of The United States. And on the other side sets the flag of Louisiana.

Setting behind his desk in a trance he watches as the street lights begin to flicker on and a steady misty rain begins falling and streaking the big oval window.

Kicking his office chair back and placing both feet on top of his big Oak wooden desk. Sheriff Thomas starts thinking about all that's happen in the last few months.

He keeps trying to wrap his mind around all these problems. And now it seems the biggest problem of all will be trying to figure out a way to defeat Mars Geophones. While destroying his Moonshine Still and arresting him and his son Link, and doing all this while not getting anyone killed in the process. Even now he's having second thoughts about asking Big George for his help. Let along the help of his grandson and the use of Lady to help find Link before he can use that A.K.-47 on someone.

CHAPTER 94

"**A**hhh... the pleasures of command," A voice says at the doorway of Sheriff Thomas's office.

Casting his gaze at the doorway Sheriff Thomas spies Deputy Lee leaning up against the door jamb with a grin on his reddish face.

"Come in Lee and grab a chair. You just might be the man who has the answers to the questions I have."

Standing six foot even with a slim built Deputy Lee is known in the department as an easy going person with a quick smile. "What every happened I didn't do it and I haven't a clue who did it and I'm standing on the Fifth Amendment," Deputy Lee says with a big smile on his face.

Cracking a grin Sheriff Thomas replies, "It's not that bad.

Didn't you serve a hitch in Vietnam in the early seventy Lee?"

Squinting his eyes, Lee replies, "Yes Sir."

"Good...have you ever hear of a device called a Geo-phone while you were over there?"

"Yea... I believe the Army used those to salt an area

where they thought there was a heavy concentration of North Vietnam troop movement. They would drop thousands of them from airplanes and set up a listening posts. And if a group of people walked close to these Geophones the Army would hear their foot falls and that would tell them which way they're travelling."

"That's what I've heard. Apparently these devices are super sensitive."

"They are sheriff. It was about the only way the Army could tell if the V.C. {Viet-Cong} were moving south of the thirty-eight parallel."

"Have you ever heard of a way to disarm a Geophone?"

Shaking his head Lee answers, "Not to my knowledge. Maybe Doyle, or Pete might know of away."

Swinging his feet off the desk and standing up Sheriff Thomas stretches his long arms over his head. "When you see them, ask them to report to me if you please."

Turning around to leave Deputy Lee says, "I'll do it sheriff."

After Deputy Lee left. Sheriff Thomas gazes at the big white faced wall clock with the block Roman numerals and mutters to himself, "Dam 3:15 in the morning."

CHAPTER 95

Getting into his all white squad car Sheriff Thomas takes his time driving down the streets of Oberlin.

With a steady drizzle of rain falling the streets give off a yellow glow where the street lights shine on the roadway.

Turning left onto E. Street Sheriff Thomas drives up to a Ranch Style brick home he bought ten years ago when he married his high school sweet heart.

Letting out a soft chuckle and thinking back. Sheriff Thomas remembers he had just graduated from the Police Academy and was ready to save the world. And protect the innocence. But after a year on the police force he and his partner got a fight in progress call one cold and rainy night. And a run in with a doped up man with a gun in a bar room fight changed his outlook on humanity. He had to take a human life to save his partner and himself.

Sheriff Thomas notice his wife Jean left the yellow porch light on for him. He knows his supper is in the oven and his glass of milk is in the icebox. Lately his suppers are a one person affair. And the love between Jean and him is reaching a cold temperature.

He remembers one night in a heated argument Jean saying, "The kids are asking, "Mommy, who's that man who comes and goes out of our house?"

After eating his plate of chicken Jambalaya Sheriff Thomas places his plate and glass in the kitchen sink.

After turning the kitchen light out he eases the bedroom door open. He's decided to undress in the dark and slid under the covers. While lying on his back and listening to Jean breathing he can tell she's not asleep. Rolling over onto his side and pulling the cover up over his shoulder he closes his eyes and prays for sleep.

CHAPTER 96

"You still asleep Old Lady of mine?" Big George whispers in the dark.

"Yes I am. And in another thirty minutes Sammy will be doing his thing my Old Man."

Sitting at the head of the kitchen table with a big white plate with two eggs fried over easy and a big kitchen spoon of Grits. Topped off with a tea spoon of homemade yellow butter and two slices of toast with grape jelly on top Big George also has his big Navy mug full of coffee. With a teaspoon of cream skimmed off a bowl of fresh cow's milk. Big George is looking at Gracie as he says, "I had a visit with Sheriff Thomas yesterday afternoon."

Without turning around from the stove Gracie replies, "That was nice of him to pop in and have a visit with you."

Wiping his mouth with a napkin Big George says, "Well…it was more than a visit."

"Ok… I'll bite Old Man. What did the sheriff want?"

Taking a pull on his coffee and setting his mug back

down Big George says, "It seems that Mars and Link are still on the sheriffs Shit List. And he may need Little George and Lady's help in getting Link."

Turning around and gazing at her husband seated at the kitchen table Gracie ask, "Now explain to me how on earth can a seventeen year old one legged old boy and a three legged dog help catch two Jelly Heads the law can't arrest."

Placing his napkin by the side of his plate Big George looks up at Gracie and says, "The sheriff seems to think Lady knows Link's scent, because she was around him when he threaten Little George and Judy."

"Why don't the sheriff just drive up to Mars old shack and put the handcuffs on him and Link. And haul both of them Knott Heads off to jail."

"It's not quite that simple Gracie. That drug runner Carl gave the sheriff some valuable information about how Mars has the woods around his place full of these Geophone."

"What kind of phones?"

"From what the sheriff told me these little "Doo-Dads"' can hear a person walking through the woods. And he thinks this is why the law has never been able to catch Mars and that boy of his doing anything wrong,"

Gracie mutters, "All because of these little Doo-Dads phones?"

"That's it my Old Lady. And it's also why he might need our help."

"Who's help?" Little George says from the kitchen doorway.

All most tipping his big Navy mug over Big George says, "Don't you know it's not polite to sneak up on your grandparents while they're talking and plotting?"

"I'm sorry Grandpa. I didn't think you were saying anything important," Little George replies. All the while he's giving his Grandma a wink.

"Have a seat and I'll tell you all about it," Big George says.

After a forty-five minute explanation of what Sheriff Thomas told him about what needed to be done to arrest the Noah's. Big George takes a big pull on his coffee mug. Then he sets it down and gazes at his Grandson and ask, "Well... what do you think of that plan?"

Taking a sip of his coffee milk Little George replies, "Sounds a little iffy to me, but I'm sure the sheriff knows what he is doing."

"Oh he does. And that's why he's going over his plan with a fine tooth comb," Gracie replies setting down at the kitchen table with a slice of left over cornbread and a bowl of milk and sugar.

CHAPTER 97

Hearing something buzzing like a bee trapped inside a jar Sheriff Thomas reaches out and hits the stop button on his alarm clock. Rolling over and setting up on the side of the bed. He knows it's just a matter of time. And he'll have to sit down with his wife and explain what's going on.

Looking at himself in the bathroom mirror Sheriff Thomas is surprised at the dark circles under his eyes and the amount of white showing in his beard. "Maybe after I get the Noah bunch locked up. I need to take a long vacation," He said to the image looking back at him in the mirror.

After getting dressed in his uniform and checking his 9Mm. Glock. Sheriff Thomas walks into the kitchen where he spies Jean standing by the washing machine putting clothes in it.

Hearing his foot falls behind her Jean glances over her shoulder and ask, "How did you sleep?"

"Ok I guess. But I could use at least twenty more hours,"

"You need to slow down Daryl. This job will kill you and our marriage. Why not let some of your deputies take a little load for you. Isn't that their job?" Jean says in a heated voice.

Looking at his beautiful wife Daryl Thomas replies,

"Yes… and in a few days this is going to be all over. And the first thing on my list of things to do is take a two week vacation. Then it's off to Florida for us."

"Promise," Jean says with a big smile and a sparkle in her eyes.

Wrapping both arms around Jean's slim waist and pulling her to him. He looks down at her soft brown eyes and says, "It's a promise." Then he bends his head down and gives her a soft kiss on the lips. He can feel a warm feeling starting to spread throughout his body.

"I guess I better go to work before I start something I can't finish."

"I know we can't finish. I hear little feet on the floor right now."

CHAPTER 98

Parking behind the Court House and taking the steps up to his second floor office, Sheriff Thomas walks through the doorway of his office and finds a note on his desk.

The note is from Deputy Lee saying he's talked to Doyle and Pete. And neither one knows of a way to render the Geophones inoperable.

Reaching for the shiny black phone in the middle of his desk Sheriff Thomas picks up the receiver and punches in the number to the downstairs jail.

After two ring's a deputy sheriff jailer picks up the phone. "This is Sheriff Thomas. Ask Lee, Doyle, and Pete to come up to my office."

After a five minute wait a voice at the door says, "You want us sheriff?"

Looking up from some of last night's paper work Sheriff Thomas mutters, "Yes...come in. And grab a seat gentlemen. I need some advice on a big problem I'm having."

As the men pull their chairs out and plop down. They

gave each other a small sideways glance.

After the men settle down Sheriff Thomas sets the paper work down he's looking at. Gazing at his three deputies Sheriff Thomas says, "The reason for this little get together is to come up with a plan to arrest Mars and Link Noah. While destroying that Moonshine Still and accomplishing all of this without getting anyone hurt, or killed. Any of you have any idea's gentlemen?"

The first to speak up is Doyle a twenty year employee of the Sheriff Department, "We've talked it over about those Geophones. The only way to deal with them is to find them. But the big problem in finding the Geophones is. How can a person search for the Geophones without Mars hearing you tromping around in the woods while you're hunting for the Geophones?

So we put our heads together and came up with a plan," Doyle says.

"I'm all ear's men," Sheriff Thomas replies looking at his men.

"The only way to get to Mars is to find out when he takes a break away from his listening station. And to get to Link our best idea is to come from the creek side. And get him when he's getting ready to leave for the day," Doyle says.

Gazing at his three deputies Sheriff Thomas cracks a smile. "I think we can make this work. I'll see if I can borrow the Grasshopper for a few days. This way Mr. Hambone can fly over Mars place and see if he can catch old Mars standing outside taking a break and at what time."

"What about Link?" Pete ask.

"I think I've got that covered. I talked to Big George the other day. And he thinks we can hike in from the other side of the creek without Link being the wiser. Once we establish his quitting time, and which tree he's hiding in. I can develop a plan to get to Link without losing anyone."

All three men look at each other with smiles on their faces. And Deputy Lee says, "I believe we got a good plan sheriff."

"The down fall of the Noah gang is at hand," Deputy Pete says with a big grin.

"But first we need to get our timing right men. Then a little practice will go a long way to insure everyone comes out of this alive," Sheriff Thomas says.

CHAPTER 99

Walking over to the table Little George is studying on. Big George claps his grandson on the shoulder. "You and Lady want to take a little ride this afternoon?"

"I guess so. Sheriff Thomas called?"

"Yea...I told Sheriff Thomas we'd meet him on the old Turner Road where you turn off to go to the Fire Tower."

Looking at the brass clock on the desk Little George said, "We better get a move on. I'll go get Lady out of the back room."

"Good while you do that. I'll fill us a canteen full of water and grab a couple of fried Bologna Sandwiches. Just in case, we get hungry on this stakeout."

After everyone loads up, Big George points the truck east on Highway Twenty Six. Once on the road Little George gazes over at his Grandpa. "Looks like dark is setting in"

"That's just what we want. The Evening Star is just coming up. And in another hour the moon will creep up above the trees. Hopefully by that time we should be in position across the creek from Mars Moonshine Still."

CHAPTER 100

Turner Road

T urning left off the highway onto a dirt and gravel road, Little George spies a wooden sign with a white painted face and big bold black letters showing "Turner Road'" on top and at the bottom "Tower Road 5 Miles.'"

Once on Turner Road all a person's eyes can see are pine trees for miles. And on the right hand side of the road is the boundary line for 65,000 acres of West Bay Game Reserve.

After a few short minutes Little George says, "I think I see a dark car park on the right side of the road Grandpa,"

Clicking the trucks high head light beams on to see better Grandpa George replies, "I see it now."

Pulling up to the car Big George doused the truck lights.

Waking up to Big George's truck, Sheriff Thomas ask, "How are you folks doing this evening, and Lady too?"

"She's ready to go sheriff," Little George says.

"And I'm ready to go too," Big George replies.

Leaning on the driver's side window Sheriff Thomas says, "I brought Deputy Lee alone just in case we run into trouble. Also we got a pair of night vision binoculars to help us out in spotting how Link gets back home, because from the Grasshopper we were able to get a leaving time on him, but not his mode of travel."

Looking up Big George says, "Well its twilight men. I guess we better hit the woods if we plan on being in our spot, when Link leaves."

"Before we go make sure you don't have any shinny objects on you, or anything that will make a noise," Sheriff Thomas says.

After checking their pockets and checking their clothing, it's decided everything is a go.

Twenty minutes into their hike Sheriff Thomas whispers, "How much further Big George?"

"We got another half a mile to go sheriff. There's a bend in this old creek bed and once we round that bend. We'll be about fifty yards from the creek bank. From there we should have a bird's eye view of Mars Moonshine Still and Links hiding place."

"That's what I need," Sheriff Thomas replies.

Looking behind himself Deputy Lee ask, "How's Lady doing Little George?"

"The way she's acting I think she may be thinking we're trying to tree raccoons."

The Old Grass Lake bed is ten feet deeper than the land surrounding it. And the sides and the bottom is made up of sugar white sand. The few bushes growing in the bottom are small with Fox Grapes covering the branches. And the rim of the Old Grass Lake is hidden by Water Oaks, White Oaks and Willow trees, thus making it hard to locate by air.

Raising his hand and pointing Big George whispers, "Everybody stop. There's our point of reference, that leaning Red Oak tree."

Sheriff Thomas says in a soft voice, "Gather around men. Once we round the bend. I want Deputy Lee to crawl up the side of the sandbar. Once on top using the Night Vision Binocular I need him to try and locate Link. While he does that I'll crawl a little ways upstream and try to find a good spot to lunch a canoe."

"What do you want Little George, Lady, and me to do?"

"I need you guy's to keep the time, when Lee spots Link and his location. Along with the direction he leaves out from. Also give me all the land marks that you can George, because we'll be making our arrest in the dark."

After the sheriff crawls away Deputy Lee eases up the ten foot tall sandbar. Big George and his crew ease away. And station themselves fifty yards downstream.

The only sound's a person's ears can detect in the dark is the noise of swirling water slapping around the old trees, which have fallen into the creek and every once in a while the croaking of a lonely Bull Frog echo's alone the shore line.

"How much longer are we going to stay put Grandpa?"

"About another five minutes should do it,"

After an eight minute wait Sheriff Thomas whispers, "Yo... come on down. We got what we come for."

On the walk back to the parking area no one spoke a word. The woods are quiet and the only light comes from the stars. As they approach their vehicles Sheriff Thomas said, "Thanks for showing us the way George. I still may need Lady's help. From what Lee was able to see tonight there seems to be more than one hollowed out tree Link may be using."

"We'll do whatever we can to help you out sheriff," Big George said.

Looking down at Little George and Lady, Sheriff Thomas says, "Your dog just might be the ticket to putting old Mars and his son behind bars and getting that Moonshine off the streets."

Feeling a glow starting to grow deep inside Little George replies, "She's a good dog sheriff. And I know she can help you out."

Reaching down and patting Lady on the head Sheriff Thomas says, "Let me get my men together and come up with a plan. Then I'll give you a call."

CHAPTER 101

O n the ride back home no one said a word. Easing up on the gas pedal Big George turns left onto Cherry Grove Road. After a short ride he turns again and bounces over the wooden Cattle Guard leading to his home. Gracie's left the back porch light on for them.

As they walk up the back steps Gracie calls out from the back door, "I got the cow milked and the eggs picked. But I didn't throw hay to the cattle, because that Brahma Bull is acting up again."

"I'll get it done," Big George yells back.

"When you two are through come on in and eat your supper," Gracie says.

After twenty minutes of feeding the cattle and washing up. Grandpa George and Little George come in and set at the table. Looking at her husband and grandson Gracie ask, "Well what's the game plan?"

"Well from what the sheriff said before we left. We have no plan," Big George replies.

Gracie laid her fork down on her plate and gazes across the table at Big George. "Why I though all this creeping you all done tonight was to find a way to lock up them Noah's."

"It is grandma. Now the sheriff has to put all that he gathered tonight together and come up with a game plan."

After Little George brushes and feeds Lady he opens the front porch screen door for her to sleep on her matt. She's gotten use to sleeping there and waking him in the morning, when it's time to get up.

Stretching out and laying on his back with his hands behind his head. Little George can hear Lady let out a soft whimper every now and then. Hearing this he mumbles to himself, "I guess she has bad dreams at times like humans."

Rolling over and looking out the bed room window. Little George's mind replays the letter he received from the L.S.U. School of Medicine. When he showed his Grandpa George the letter he spied a smile a country mile wide on his face. Even Judy was glad, when he told her the good news. After a short time of just staring out the window and listening to the silence of the night Little George's eyes submitted to the peace and quiet of the dark.

CHAPTER 102

Lying back to back in their bed and trying with all their might to fall asleep Big George and Gracie are not gaining on their quest for a goodnights sleep. Finally Gracie ask, "George do you think this job of arresting Mars and that Jelly Head son of his will be dangerous?"

"Well it want be like going to church if that's what bothering you."

"I'm just worried about Little George. I don't want him to see something terrible happen and him have a relapse. He's been doing great these last few months and Lady has helped him a lot."

"Don't worry Old Lady of mine. I got that covered."

Pulling the blankets up to her neck Gracie replies, "Ok my Old Man good night."

Laying in the dark Gracie knows the loss of their only grandchild would be too much for her and George to bear. It was bad enough to loss their only son, and a daughter-in-law they'd seen raised in the neighborhood. And the loss of a beautiful granddaughter with so much life left to live weight's heavy on Gracie's heart. And now with the problem of Little George being involved in a dangerous arrest Gracie wonders.

Rolling over and facing the window Gracie can see the North Star. Saying a short prayer she closes her eyes.

CHAPTER 103

When the old court house clock in the tower struck 7:00 in the morning Sheriff Thomas is already on his third cup of coffee, when in walks his hand-picked deputies. After a few cups of coffee everyone sat down at the sheriff's oval shaped mahogany conference table. On the table are stacks of photos the pilot of the Grasshopper has taken. And the Timing Chart of Mars movement. Along with the surveillance charts Sheriff Thomas and Deputy Lee filled out on their night of creeping with Big George and Little George.

"Everybody got a pencil and paper?" Sheriff Thomas said looking at each man.

When everyone nodded ok Sheriff Thomas says, "This arrest may be a tough one. But the first thing I want to stress is safety first and no heroics. Just good old fashion police work. We'll try to take Mars and his son alive. As all of you know these two birds march to a different drum beat. If they aim their weapon at you then you do whatever it takes to neutralize the situation."

Deputy Lee ask, "Even if it means having to shoot somebody?"

Sheriff Thomas looks at Deputy Lee as he replies, "That's exactly what I mean. In the photos in front you you'll see Mars heading for an Outhouse. And the time on the bottom of the photo shows 4:00 in the evening. Now he's done this three days in a row."

"So this leads you to believe he's away from his listening post at this time of the day?" Deputy Doyle ask.

"This is what I'm hoping it shows Doyle. After his break we now see him rolling a cigarette and taking a leisurely walk. But here's the kicker. He's on the move. And he only stays about five minutes in the Out House. So in that time frame we have to be on top of him."

"Wow... that's not much time to get to him sheriff," Deputy Pete mumbles.

"You're right on that Pete. Not if you go in on foot."

Everyone seated at the table looks at one another then hunches their shoulders.

Seeing the looks of dismay on his deputy's faces Sheriff Thomas ask, "You guys remember the white truck the drug runners had?"

"Yea... I remember it," Deputy Leo replies.

"Well that's going to be our wracking ram. When old Mars closes the door to the Out House, we want to knock him and the Out House over."

After the laughter subsides the sheriff says, "This is the only thing I can come up with to get to Mars fast and without any gun play."

"I'll drive the truck sheriff," Deputy Leo says wiping a tear with his shirt sleeve.

"Ok… that'll work. Leo will drive the truck and I want two deputies in the back of the truck with rifles to back him up just in case."

CHAPTER 104

After the men have their sip of coffee. Sheriff Thomas clears his throat. "Now the hard one... Mr. Link Noah... Deputy Lee and Big George and Little George alone with Lady and myself did a little creeping last night. What we found out is Link uses several camouflaged trees to conceal himself. And the worst part of it is you don't know, which tree he is in.

And his habits seem to be an everyday thing. Old Link heads to the Moonshine Still at about 4:00 in the morning on a black four wheeler. Once he has the Moonshine Still up and running. He'll hide in one of the three fake trees. During the day he moves around checking the Moonshine Still and taking care of Mother Nature's calling. Then about dark we see him get back on the black three wheeler and he heads back home."

"Is this were Lady comes in?" Deputy Lee ask.

"You got it Lee. We know she has his scent. But the only thing I'm worry about is once she tags him. We need to be on top of Link. Otherwise he might start shooting."

"What about Big George and Little George?" Deputy Pete ask.

"My plan is that Little George and Lady stays with me. And Big George and Deputy Lee keep us covered from across the creek."

"Lots of luck with that plan sheriff," Deputy Doyle says.

Sheriff Thomas gazes at Deputy Doyle as he says, "My plan for capturing Link is a little more complicated. There will be two groups of deputes in two inflated rafts. We'll put in about a mile above the Mill House bend. And drift with the current till we reach the bluff where the Moonshine Still is located."

"What if Link has no plan in giving up peacefully," Deputy Leo ask.

Sheriff Thomas shifts his gaze to Deputy Leo and says, "Like I said early. Once we identify ourselves. It's up to Link whether he lives, or not. I don't want any hero's on this mission. Everybody got that."

Everyone seated at the table nods their head in agreement.

"When are we executing the warrant sheriff?" Deputy Lee ask.

"Two nights from now, but tonight we'll have a couple of dry runs. And tomorrow night I'll bring in our civilian counter parts. And get them use to our mode of operation."

CHAPTER 105

Installing a heavy duty front bumper on the front of the white pickup trunk the drug runners used and the loan of a portable toilet. Sheriff Thomas ran his men through a timed course starting one mile away from the portable toilet.

The plan consist of two deputies standing up in the rear of the pickup with automatic rifles and a driver.

The timed course starts once the pickup starts in motion. And Sheriff Thomas starts his time watch. The first timed run came in at one and a half minutes. Not satisfied with the run Sheriff Thomas said, "No good men. I need you to put your foot through the floor board Pete."

On the next run through the men completed the course in just under a half a minute. "Looking good now guys. Now I need my water assault team and my sniper," The Sheriff says.

"How are we going to drill this out without water, or rafts?" Deputy Doyle ask.

"I got that covered Doyle. Everybody load up in your cars and follow me to the Calcasieu River Bridge. Everything we need is waiting there for us."

CHAPTER 106

Calcasieu River Bridge

Heading west on Highway Twenty-Six and turning off onto a sandy dirt road, which runs parallel to the bridge. The sheriff and his deputies decide to park under the bridge.

There waiting for them are four retired Special Forces veterans. The big boned man in black Army Fatigues walks up and says, "Well… well what are you boys doing out so late,"

"If you don't know, I'm not telling," Deputy Lee replies.

Sheriff Thomas walks up to the men. "Ok everyone knows everyone. So let's get this dog and pony show on the road."

Once a target is place at the estimated distance with a mockup of a man about the size of Link Noah. A big burly man by the name of Jack Lemon appears out of nowhere carrying a black case. Walking up to Deputy Lee he says, "So you the man Sheriff Thomas calls the best shot in his department."

Jack Lemon spent time in the Navy as a Seal doing

three hitches in Vietnam. After a time Jack opted out of the navy for personal reasons.

Looking this man over Deputy Lee estimates Jack's age to be close to sixty. His long dark straight hair is streaked with gray. And a gray handlebar mustache covers his upper lip. Perched under a brow of bushy dark eyebrows is a set of sky blue eyes. "I guess if the sheriff say's so then I'm it," Deputy Lee replies.

Laying a black leather case softly on the sand bar, Jack pops open the two clips that hold the case shut. Then gingerly his big hands pick up a black rifle with a scope mounted on top. Jack Looks at Deputy Lee as he says, "What you're looking at Deputy Lee is a XM25 Navy Weapon System. This black beauty is a 308 caliber rifle with a range of 983 yards. But you'll be shooting about seventy to eighty yards."

Handing the rifle to Deputy Lee with a clip, Jack explains the operation of the weapon system. "Got any question for me Deputy Lee?"

Holding the rifle in his hands and feeling the warmth of the weapon Deputy Lee ask, "I have only one question. How on earth did you get a hold of a weapon like this?"

Jack gazes at Lee with a pair of eyes that show this man has lived and seen too much in his life time. Slowly Jack replies, "This is "My Piece"' Deputy Lee and you're the only person this side of hell that's every touched it."

Looking into the face of this man Deputy Lee feels a cold chill run up his spine. Because he knows this is as close to death as he'll ever be in his life time.

"Ready to try out Little Betsy Deputy Lee?"

"Might as well," Deputy Lee replies.

As they reach the end of the sand bar Jack ask, "Which shooting position are you comfortable with Deputy Lee?"

"I'll use the Prone Position."

A slight smile creases Jack's face as he replies, "I kinda like that position myself. But before we start let me give you a little advice on killing a person."

Hearing this remark catches Deputy Lee off guard. For some unknown reason he has it in his mind he's not going to kill Link. Maybe not even fire the rifle, "Ok." Deputy Lee chocks out.

Sensing the change in Deputy Lee's voice Jack continues, "There are two kill spots on a person. Number one is a head shot. And the other is a heart shot. Of course if you want to disable the enemy you can go for a shoulder shot, or a hip shot. This is solely the shooter decision."

Looking at the mockup on the other side of the river Deputy Lee replies, "I understand."

Further upstream a group of men are lunching two military inflatable rafts into the water. "All right men," A slim built man named Roy Adams says. "Here's the "Straight Skinny'" on navigating on the water. Your right side is the "Starboard Side'" and your left side is your "Portside.'" Everybody got that part?"

Roy Adams stayed in the Navy for thirty years and made the rank of Senior Chief Boatswain Mate. Standing 6ft.2in Roy ruled the main decks of a Destroyer.

Seeing the confused look on his men's faces Sheriff Thomas says, "Maybe we can skip the Navy terminology for now Roy."

Shrugging his shoulders Roy replies, "Alright men this is how we're going to work this out. The two men in the front and the two in the back will row at the same time. I'm in the very back and I'll be your rudder. The secret to sneaking up on some-one is to simply plant your paddles strait down into the water. Then pull back in one slow motion. Whatever you do don't slap the water with you paddle. Any question before we shove off?"

Everyone looks at each other. But no one said a word.

Once the inflatable rafts are in the water they easily skim on top of the dark water in a soundless motion. The men can only hear their own breathing and the water lapping the sides of the inflated rafts.

After a mile of coasting Roy says, "I'm going to beach us on that big sand bar on our starboard side. Then one of you can take a turn at being the rudder man."

Back at the target Jack whispers, "Ok Lee take a deep breath and squeeze the trigger. Put one shot right "Between his Running Lights,"'

Deputy Lee looks sideways at Jack. "Between his what?"

With a grin on his face Jack says, "His eyes Lee. I'm sorry. I forgot I'm dealing with a Land Lubber."

Deputy Lee takes a deep breath and places his eye brow gently against the scoop. As he exhales he slowly squeezes the trigger.

He feels the rifle kick back against his right shoulder. But to his surprise it feels like a soft tap.

The first shot scores a perfect hit. "Humm-hum. That's a good hit if I do say so myself. Now try a right shoulder hit then a right hip shot."

Once the shots are completed Jack mumbles, "Yep... that'll work Deputy Lee. You got the hang of it."

Holding the rifle in both hands Lee says, "This is one

sweet shooting rifle."

"It's yours to use Deputy Lee. Just take good care of "Little Betsy."' And don't let anyone else touch My Peace."

The sun has set. And the Lighting Bugs are dancing in the Willow trees as the last raft is pulled up onto the sand bar. Sheriff Thomas gathers his men up close and says, "This is our first training with the rafts and using a sniper. Tomorrow night I'll bring Big George and his grandson. Along with Lady for our final training then it's off for the real thing."

"You need us back here tomorrow night?" Roy Adams ask.

Gazing in Roy's direction Sheriff Thomas replies, "I sure would like it if you boys could just in case I miss something."

"We'll be here about "Dark-Thirty,"' Jack Green says.

CHAPTER 107

Walking into his office and plopping down on his old black leather office chair, Sheriff Thomas spies a white envelope with a hand written note in black ink that reads "Have Fun." Slicing the paper open he shakes out five tickets to a large amusement park in Orlando Florida for seven days and nights. Smiling Sheriff Thomas places the tickets into his top shirt pocket.

Standing up and rubbing his aching back Sheriff Thomas walks over to the coffee pot and pours a generous amount of thick black coffee into his blue mug.

Walking back to his desk he picks up the black phone receiver and punches in Big George's home phone number. On the second ring a voice on the other end says, "Hello."

"George… this is Sheriff Thomas. How are you doing this great and beautiful evening?"

"Why… hello there sheriff, I'm doing just fine. I was waiting to hear from you."

"I just wanted to inform you we had a dry run with a couple of old buddies of mine late this afternoon."

"How did it go?" Big George ask.

"Better than I expected to tell you the truth. Now I need you and Little George alone with Lady to meet up with us tomorrow evening late at the Calcasieu Bridge. So you guys can get familiar with our mode of operation."

"Do we need to bring anything with us?"

"No… just yourselves. I want you guys to get the feel of what we're going to do and what to expect if things go wrong."

After a moment of silence Big George says, "Ok… I got you sheriff. We'll be there."

After hanging the phone up Gracie ask, "Was that who I think it was?"

"Yes it was my Old Lady."

"Well I'm headed for a hot bath. Then the roost,"

"Let out a whoop when you're through," Big George says.

CHAPTER 108

The next morning bright and early Big George calls a family meeting, looking at his wife and his grandson. "This afternoon the sheriff want's Little George and me along with Lady to meet up with him and his deputies at the Calcasieu Bridge. And from what he said they must be practicing to go in and arrest Mars and Link."

"He must think this is a real dangers arrest," Gracie says.

Holding his breath Little George says "Maybe he wants everybody to know what to do. That way they're not running over each other."

"That's what I think," Big George replies.

CHAPTER 109

As the hands on the big black and white United Clock hanging on the wall slowly moves. Lady and Little George stay busy at Grandpa George's clinic.

Little George is helping Judy dip a dog and Lady is checking on a kitten that was found roaming around in the woods alone Flat Creek.

As they work. Little George can see the concern in Judy's eyes. "You and Lady better be careful Little George. Those two "Knot Heads'" are dangerous when they're in a good mood. Let along when somebody is trying to arrest them."

"Don't worry we'll be careful."

CHAPTER 110

L ittle George can hear his Grandpa George calling him, "Little George get Lady we need to saddle up and hit the dusty trail."

Hopping up onto the seat Lady's tail is wagging ninety miles an hour. Grandpa George twist the key. And the truck engine roars to life.

As they turned onto the highway Grandpa George gazes over at Little George seated by the passenger side door and ask, "You a little nervous?"

"Just a little bit for you and me. But a lot for Lady,"

As they reach the bridge that spans the Calcasieu River. Big George turns off the highway and drives down towards the river.

They are surprised to see all the people and equipment. "Wow... I didn't know the cavalry is on this mission," Grandpa George says.

Once all the introductions are done. Sheriff Thomas divides the men into three groups.

Grandpa George is with Deputy Lee. And Lady and Little George are with Sheriff Thomas's group.

And the third group is made up of deputies with the old white truck the drug runners used.

After two hours of jumping in and out the rafts. And running up a bluff bank and letting Lady find an old shirt of Link's. Sheriff Thomas decides it's time to call for a break.

After a big stainless steel coffee maker is empty. Sheriff Thomas calls a meeting at the water's edge. "Tonight we made a big improvement in our timing and I don't think we can do any better. Early this morning I checked with the weather station in Lake Charles and they're predicting three days of rain starting day after tomorrow. So that leaves us with tomorrow night as a window of opportunity for us to get in and take care of business. Is there any objection to this plan?"

"Let's make it ago sheriff. I believe we're ready," Deputy Pete says.

"Good. Then we go at twilight tomorrow. And now I'd like to give a big thinks to our senior Special Forces people who helped train us."

After the talk dies down and the equipment is loaded. Big George wonders over where Little George and Lady are sharing a Peanut Butter and Grape Jelly sandwich. "Are you two ready to hit the saw dust trail?"

CHAPTER 111

All the way home all is quite in the truck. The only noise comes from Lady's breathing and the "Mud Grip Tires'" rolling on the asphalt road.

After Grandpa George and Little George get home. And after feeding and brushing Lady. Little George walks in through the kitchen doorway.

Standing there for a few short minutes he can tell his grandpa and grandma have been in a heated discussion. If he was a betting person, Little George would say it's about him being involved in that mission tomorrow night.

Noticing Little George standing in the doorway Grandma Gracie says, "Have a seat Little George and I'll get you a plate of "Chicken Fricassee'" and a glass of milk."

Grandpa George puts his fork down and gives Little George his best stare as he says, "You're grandma and I have been talking about the danger in having you involved in this arrest that's going down tomorrow night. And being that you're the only grandchild that we have if something should go wrong and you get hurt. I don't know what we'd do."

Little George can tell by the look in their eyes, that the concern for his safety is number one with them.

After a few short minutes pasts Little George says, "I'll stay out of the way. It's Lady that'll be the one in harm's way."

"That's true, but you never know what to expect from Link. Why if he should say Good Morning to you. A body better go outside and look. It just might be storming," Grandpa George replies.

"I'll say. I don't think the boy's elevator goes all the way to the top floor," Grandma Gracie says.

"It's kind of late for me to just up and pull out. Without Lady's help the sheriff doesn't have a clue which tree Link will be hiding in. And the sheriff needs Lady to tap the tree that Link's hiding in. Otherwise he may lose a deputy if he starts shooting."

After Little George has his say it's so quiet and still in the kitchen you can hear water dripping in the sink.

Finally Grandma Gracie says, "All I got to say about this is you better be careful young man."

Then she gets up and goes into the living room leaving Grandpa George and Little George setting at the table staring at each other.

CHAPTER 112

Being sheriff of Allen Parish has its moments of excitement and its days of routine everyday problems. Lately life for Sheriff Thomas has been one long pain in the britches with the F.B.I. digging into every nook-an-cranny looking for more evidence. Now Interpol has gotten into the act. But the only thing on his mind now is to arrest the Noah's. And take his family on a much needed vacation while he still has a wife.

Pulling up the driveway and parking his squad car under a Pecan Tree. Sheriff Thomas doused the head lights and turns the key to the off position.

Reaching over the top of the dashboard he picks up the white envelope containing the tickets. Walking into the kitchen he spies Jean standing over the sink rinsing a baby bottle.

Hearing her husband's foot falls behind her Jean says, "Welcome back home cowboy."

From the tone of her voice he knows his time away from his family has been hard on her and not fair by a long shot. But he knows it's time for him to pay attention to his family. "I got a little surprise for you."

Slowly turning around and gazing in his direction she ask, "What surprise?"

Sheriff Thomas waves the envelope up in the air and

says, "I got us one whole week in Orlando, Florida. No phones, or beepers, and no radios. How's that for a vacation?"

With tears welling up in her eyes Jean throws her arms around her husband's neck and whispers in his ear, "You promise."

"Boy Scouts honor."

After a big supper of Purple Hull Peas with Stake and Gravy, Sheriff Thomas spends time with his two daughters and son watching them play and asking him question about his work. After a while Jean comes and sets down by him.

Within a few seconds he picks up his favorite perfume smell. Glancing sideways at Jean he spies a big smile on her face.

After the kids have their bath he lays on his back looking up at the white ceiling of their bedroom.

As Jean gets in bed beside him she lays her head on his chest and whispers, "Got any plans for tonight cowboy?"

Looking into her deep blue eyes he whispers, "I sure do Mrs. Thomas."

CHAPTER 113

Fire Tower Road

After a long day of doing nothing but watching the clock and the sun Little George hears his Grandpa George calling him, "Come on Little George we need to hit the road. The sheriff and his men will be waiting for us at The Old Fire Tower Road."

On the drive to their meeting place both Grandpa George and Little George seem lost in their own thoughts and neither said a word. As they drive up to a bunch of sheriff cars and trucks Little George spies Sheriff Thomas heading their way.

Sticking his head into the window Sheriff Thomas says, "Glad to see you guys."

Big George steps out first. "How are we going to break up sheriff?"

"Let's all gather around over here and I'll explain to everyone what my plan is all about."

After the men quiet down the sheriff opens a map on the hood of his squad car.

Looking around at his men he says, "Pete you take Leo and

Doyle with you and once you get on station with the old truck stay put until you hear from me."

Pete shifts his hat backwards and says, "Got you sheriff."

Looking around at Big George, "You go with Deputy Lee. You'll be his spotter and our eyes in case something goes wrong."

Big George looks at Deputy Lee. "I'm ready when you are. We got a little walking to do before we get there."

Picking up the black case that holds the rifle, Deputy Lee says, "Lead on Mr. George."

Sheriff Thomas looks at the remaining nine men. "Let's load up men we got a little drive to our spot."

Sheriff Thomas looks at Little George." You and Lady will ride with me,"

After a ride of a mile the men turn off the gravel road onto an old logging trail.

After another mile they came up on what the locals call "The Old Gas Camp'" that's been abandon for years. The Old Gas Camp was used to house and feed Pipe Liners back in the nineteen-forty's when a thirty-two inch main pipeline was laid under the creek bed. The Old Camp consist of a cook's shack and a bunkhouse for the men to sleep in and a small building for repairs.

After reaching the sight the men pour out of the trucks.

In a matter of a few short minutes the two inflatable rafts are shoved down the bluff bank and onto the white sand bar. Once the paddles and weapons are loaded a quick check is made. The rafts are then shoved off the sandbar and onto the cold spring fed waters of Whisky Chitto Creek.

"The way it looks on my map we're about one mile upstream from the Moonshine Still and Link. Ok you five take the rear boat," Sheriff Thomas says pointing his finger. "Now I want Little George and Lady with me and you four in the front of the raft. This way we'll be the lead boat."

Letting the rafts go with the eight mile an hour current, the sheriff figures it will be a fifteen minute ride to the Mill House Bend.

As soon as his feet touch the ground he has to call the men in the truck and give the go signal for them to start their run on Mars and hopefully arrest him.

The fire flies and cicadas are already starting their show and somewhere down the creek a lonely owl hoots a few times.

The sun has set and every now and then the man on the rudder has to make a quick adjustment. Because of the old trees that have fallen into the creek. At times the rafts passes close enough to the fallen trees it causes the startled turtles sleeping on the fallen trees to slip into the water.

"Hold what you got men. Here we are. When I say let Lady loose. Little George let her go but you stay with the raft.

You first five deputies run like hell behind Lady as soon as her paws hit the sand," The sheriff whispers in the dark.

Reaching for his radio that's hooked on his belt, Sheriff Thomas clicks the key down and whispers into the mic, "Run Rabbit... Run."

CHAPTER 114

Hearing the code to start their run Deputy Pete shifts the truck into first gear and yells out to the two deputies standing in the back of the truck bed, "Hold on tight back there if old Mars aims a gun at us... you know what to do."

Letting up on the clutch and pushing down on the gas pedal it takes a short two seconds for the rear tires to gain traction. Then the truck is off in a cloud of dust and gravel.

As soon the raft nudges the sandbar Little George whispers to Lady, "Go find him girl."

Hearing these words Lady shoots out of the raft and is half way up the bluff bank before Sheriff Thomas and his deputies can get a foot hold.

It takes Link about a "New York Minute'" which is fifteen seconds in Louisiana time to figure out something is wrong. Some kind of animal is outside his hiding place growling at the tree he's hiding in.

All of a sudden he hears voices yelling out loud for him to

come out and lay down on his face…Now!!"

Thinking Link might pull a fast one the sheriff sprays ten rounds from his machine gun over Links head. All the while knocking fiberglass and plaster and plastic leaves on top his head.

"One more time Link. Come out, or they're going to need a dust pan to pick you up with," Sheriff Thomas yells out.

"Ok…Ok!!! Don't shoot… I'm coming out."

"First your gun then you Link."

As Link lays on the ground one of the deputy's hand-cuffs his wrist together behind his back. While the other deputy checks him for hidden weapons. The remaining seven deputies are busy placing C-4 explosive around and under the big Moon-shine Still.

Dazed and confused Link blurts out, "What in the hell is this all about sheriff. You got no right to arrest me."

Walking up to Link the sheriff says with a big smile on his face, "Look at this piece of paper Link. It's a warrant for you and your old man."

All of a sudden a gunshot echoes through the woods and it causes Sheriff Thomas to grab his radio and key the mic down. "Talk to me Pete."

After a moment of fuzzed-up-static-filled chatter Deputy Pete's voice crackles over the radio, "We got Mars in custody sheriff. That shot you heard was Mars's shot gun going off, when we knocked the Out House over with him still inside…Over"

"Is he ok Pete?" In the back ground the sheriff can hear muffled laughter.

After a few seconds Pete comes back on the radio,

"Oh...Yes Sir, but he'll need a bath before we can book him... Over."

As the situation calms down Sheriff Thomas checks on Little George and finds Lady getting a bunch of pats on the head from his men.

A voice from across the creek yells out, "You got that Knot Head under control sheriff?"

"We got him Big George. All's well over here. If you and Lee want to head back to the Tower Road go ahead."

Once Little George and Lady are loaded back up, Sheriff Thomas waits until everybody is out of the danger zone.
He reaches into his life vest pocket and pulls out a small black squire box. Flipping a toggle switch on top the box Sheriff Thomas waits a few short seconds for a green light to appear. Once the green light appears he presses a red button on the side of the box. Within a short second the big Moonshine Still makes a lovely glow in the night sky as the C-4 explodes.

Reaching their landing spot the rafts are loaded up again. And Mars and Link are put in a sheriff's squid car and on their way to jail. Lady and Little George get to ride in Sheriff Thomas's squid car.

By the time thing are done the sun has started to peak over the tall pine trees of "West Bay." And the sheriff is still busy getting important information from his deputies for his report to the District Attorney.

Little George is on his last bite of an egg and bacon sandwich when the sheriff walks up to him. "I can't think you and Lady enough for your help. If Lady hadn't found the tree that Link was in, I might have lost a deputy, or two."

"She did all the work. I just stood by and watched," Little George says.

The next morning "The Allen Parish Tribune News Paper"' ran a report on the front page in big bold black letters reporting. MARS AND LINK NOAH ARRESTED FOR TRAFFICKING IN MOONSHINE.

CHAPTER 115

Our Home on Flat Creek

T en years has pasted since that glorious night. But from time to time Little George lets his mind wonder to that special point in time.

Now he's a Doctor of Veterinarian Medicine and works with his Grandpa George.

And Judy and he are married with two children of their own. They've made their home on his mother and father's place on the banks of Flat Creek.

Every once in a while Little George stops by the graveyard where his love ones are laid to rest just to talk things over with them. Then it's back to the clinic and back to work. Right now he can feel a wet noise poking him on his leg. Looking up at the clock hanging over his office door he can see that it's 4:30.

Looking under his desk he sees a set of brown eyes looking back at him. "Your right girl it's time to go home and check on Judy and the kids."

Lady's age is starting to slow her down a little. But she still comes to work with Little George each day. As usual the first thing she does each morning is check on every sick animal in the clinic then she takes a nap under his desk.

After her nap she'll spend her day helping out where ever she's needed. Her favorite place is setting on the seat of the truck by the open passenger window like she's doing now.

Once they're home she's out of the truck and off to find the kids and play awhile with them.

The things Little George like best about living on Flat Creek is. You don't hear police car siren's screaming all day and into the night. And, when somebody passes your house in a car they always honk the horn and wave.

If you break down on the road the first car to pass by will stop and check on you. And the young folks around Flat Creek still call the older folks uncle, or aunt even though they are not related. And you still hear yes sir and no sir. Of course the best entertainment in the world is still free. It's called "Mother Nature's Late Evening Show."'

Walking up on the front porch and hanging his hat on a wooden peg Little George eases through the kitchen doorway and spies Judy and the kid's rubbing Lady and talking to her.

He can still remember the first time he laid eyes on her. All broken up and covered in blood and dirt. "I figured you weren't far behind Lady," Judy says looking at Little George over her shoulder.

After the kids are fed and had their bath. And Lady is in her bed by the fire place. The house settles down and gets quiet. Every now and then Little George hears one of the kid's mumbling in his sleep.

A big harvest moon is shining through the bedroom window and keeps the night from being so dark. With the bed room window open he can hear a lonely owl hooting in a tree somewhere on Flat Creek.

Rolling over and putting his arm over Judy's waist. He can

feel her body heat through her thin night gown. Taking a deep breath and slowly closing his eyes Little George knows all is well on Flat Creek tonight.   THE END

AUTHOR'S NOTES

This is a work of fiction. The names of the people and the episodes are also fiction. But the names of places are real.

In the Mid-1940 a group of men formed The American Coon Hunters Association. As time went on more people joined and the competition grew. Most of the dog's that are used in The World Championship are Walker Hounds. The rules I used in this book are made up and do not reflect on the rules of the A.C.H.A.

Keep Reading

AUTHOR'S BOOKS

Murder over The Mississippi River

Murder On The Rigolets Bridge

Little George and the Grand-NiteChampion

All three books can be found at

AMAZON.COM

KEEP READING